I0831475

The Image of

Rachel Clair

Haunting Mysteries of the Old South

Book One

JUDITH M. MCMANUS

This story is a work of fiction. Any names, people, places, or circumstances are merely a product of the author's imagination or used fictitiously.

ISBN: 9781078209847

Published by Vintage South Books
Cover design by Vintage South Books
Printed in the United States of America

First edition

For JFM

PROLOGUE

MARCH 1995

"Here again, Miss Montgomery?" asked Mr. Henly, head of the Department of Archives. "This is the third time this week."

"I'm fully aware," I signed in then placed my briefcase on one of the three empty rectangular tables. "Mr. Meeks needs all the information on the Edwardian style of the large homes on Twelfth Avenue South. The ones built around 1900."

He chuckled and returned to his desk behind the small sliding glass window of his office. I seem to live at the Birmingham Public Library these days. Being an architect's assistant at Meeks and Hays meant that I had to do most of the research and legwork.

Mr. Meeks was in the process of renovating two of the lovely old homes on the Southside and planned to return the structures to their original splendor. Not an easy task without detailed records, blueprints, and photographs. Finding those was my mission today.

"It will take a few minutes to find the files. A lot of the information is on microfilm, and you can help yourself over there," Mr. Henly gestured to a large microfilm reader.

"While you're searching, I'll try the newspaper archives upstairs," I said. "Maybe I can locate some old articles with photographs from the era."

The old library building was built in 1927, and it fascinated me. The marble floors and stairs were original, and the musty smell from old volumes somehow seemed familiar to me. I gripped the brass handrail and climbed fourteen steps to the local newspaper archive. An older woman sat behind the desk.

"Excuse me. I'm interested in finding architectural photographs and articles from the turn of the century," I said.

"You'll find the older issues on microfilm. Especially from that long ago," the woman said. "The fire of 1925 destroyed some of the issues, but not all."

I nodded a 'thank you' and found a vacant microfilm reader. I started from the beginning, January 1, 1900. After two hours and no luck, I closed my eyes, turned the handle of the reel, and counted to ten. I stopped it on the date of April 15, 1909, and the headline caught my attention.

MURDER IN COAL SPRINGS
ODEN COUNTY DEPUTY SHERIFF ARRESTS SUSPECT

Coal Springs? That was only forty miles away. My family was from that part of Oden County, but I've never been there. I don't remember a murder ever mentioned. I was intrigued and had to read the short article.

APRIL 3, 1909 Coal Springs, Alabama- *The body of a young woman was found floating in Cain Creek yesterday. She had been beaten. From the looks of the murder scene, there was an apparent struggle, and the deputy sheriff has cordoned off the area for investigation. Deputy Sheriff John Crow has arrested a suspect in connection with the crime. The suspect is not originally from Coal Springs. The name of the victim has not been released.*

I looked up from the screen and wondered whose family this young woman was connected to. Could she have been related to me? With none of my family members left, I had no one to ask.

Scouring later issues for more information on the crime, I found an article on the front page of the September 5, 1909 issue of the newspaper denoting the murder trial for James Cason, the defendant. He must have been the suspect mentioned in the earlier article. The article was lengthy, and I hoped I had enough time to read it. My curiosity about the mysterious young victim had me wanting to find out every detail about her. We could be related.

THE TRIAL OF JAMES CASON by T. S. Logan
Just as it occurred on day one.

SEPTEMBER 3, 1909 Oden, Alabama *It would be redundant to go into details about the grisly crime charged against this savage brute. A young life was brutally taken away, and this trial will seal the defendant's fate. If found guilty of such a heinous felony, James Cason will most likely receive the death penalty.*

This trial has drawn most of the town of Coal Springs to Oden to witness the proceedings. The young victim was a lifelong resident there but wasn't considered an upstanding young woman. Many of the so-called elite citizens of Coal Springs have sought my attention to explain the sin and provocation of the victim. From this reporter's viewpoint, the Coal Springs elite are merely overzealous church members who want to defame the victim as much as the defendant. In my opinion, as well as other reporters covering this trial, the citizens of Coal Springs must have much to cover up by way of slandering the poor victim. The scrutiny alone is a topic for another article, which I will delve into at another time.

The rain poured as the courtroom and gallery were filled at the Oden County Courthouse. James Cason entered the room in handcuffs and leg irons...

Reluctantly, I had to stop reading and I had no time to make copies of the article. Mr. Henly was waiting for me in archives, and I had to go back to Mr. Meeks with something.

"Mr. Henly, I'm sorry," I said. "I came across an interesting headline dating back to 1909."

"About Twelfth Avenue?"

"No, about a murder in Coal Springs."

"Hardly an architectural article," he said with a chuckle.

I smiled and sat at the large table. "I had no luck finding anything about Southside in that era. What did you find?"

Mr. Henly placed a stack of folders in front of me. "These files are full of old photos and copies of original blueprints from different homes in the area at that time. There are some related photographs to the owners of the properties. I hope this will help. I made copies for you."

I looked at my watch. I had two hours to finish and get back to the office. But I couldn't stop thinking about that murdered girl and why her name was defamed and never printed. I'll come back to the library tomorrow and pick up where I left off.

I made it back to the office in plenty of time. "Mr. Meeks, here are copies of blueprints and old photographs from 1902," I said when entering my boss's office. "The house at 1764-1766 Twelfth Avenue was built that year as a duplex."

"Hmm, good work Miss Montgomery," he said.

"From what I understand, Mr. Meeks, the entire duplex was owned by a Miss Annie Smalley. She passed away at age ninety-two and left no heirs."

Mr. Meeks thumbed through the files. "It looks like Miss Smalley was from Coal Springs. Isn't that where your people are from?"

"How did I miss that?" I took the file as he handed it to me. "May I look over the file this weekend?"

"Don't forget to bring it back. We'll do a walkthrough at the duplex Monday morning to see what's salvageable," he said.

Spending another Friday night alone, I kept thinking about Coal Springs and how my family rarely spoke of it. The murdered girl, who was she? Could she have been someone Annie Smalley knew? I grabbed the file and flipped through the pictures. There was a color image of the Birmingham duplex with two elderly women standing on the front porch. The year 1978 was written on the back. One woman was white; the other was black and wearing thick glasses.

The next image was much older, torn, and yellowed. The date written on the ragged edge was 1909. There were two little girls and a young blonde woman holding a baby. I turned it over and read 'Boarding House' followed by four names: Annie, Frances, Rachel, Josie. They posed in front of an old wooden building. The next photographs were of the architecture of downtown Birmingham's older buildings.

As I read the details, I learned Miss Smalley purchased the duplex in 1946. She and Kiz Moseley lived in one side and rented out the other. Kiz must be the black woman with glasses. I looked at the clock, and it was past midnight. I couldn't sleep. I couldn't wait to scroll through the microfilm one more time.

A different woman sat behind the desk in the newspaper archives, and I took a seat at the microfilm reader. I found the article on the trial of James Cason and continued to read where I left off:

...The spectators gasp and whisper as the defendant stops at the defense table. With his head down, James Cason makes eye contact with no one. My point of observation is at the back of the courtroom where this reporter has a clear vision of the trial in its entirety.

The article ended there. Disappointed, I looked for the continuation of the article, but it was missing. I found another article related to Coal Springs, again written by T. S. Logan.

SEPTEMBER 10, 1909 *The small community of Coal Springs, Alabama is comprised of a few small stores, a sheriff's office, and a renowned hotel considered the "finest in the south to reclaim lost health."*

Due to five natural springs, the rich mineral waters in the area offer healing and comfort to elite summer vacationers. At the local swimming hole, Cain Creek, unmarried couples are forbidden to swim together. Boys are permitted to swim five days out of seven and usually in the nude. Girls may swim only on designated days, and bathing dresses are required.

A self-professed God-fearing community, the elders of the local church run the town. They make the rules and take pride in denouncing any citizen or stranger whom they considered inferior, immoral in the opinion of the church, or conduct themselves in sinful and scandalous ways. Residents considered wicked, are run out of town in disgrace by the "pillars of the community," as their former neighbors look on with ferocious disapproval and cruel condemnation. This reporter witnessed this behavior at the trial of James Cason. I interviewed unnamed residents of the community, and my observation is confirmed. I am making it my duty as a newspaper reporter to publish articles like this one to make my readers aware of senseless scrutiny placed upon fellow human beings in towns and communities everywhere.

My obsession with Coal Springs was just beginning.

PART ONE

RACHEL

CHAPTER 1

COAL SPRINGS, ALABAMA 1905

"Rachel, you'll be late for school now. I'll take you this morning."

"I'm coming, Daddy. I have to button my shoes."

Noble Clair double-checked the harness on Old General and made sure this week's cotton crop was secured tightly on the buckboard. As he surveyed his offerings, he folded his arms, nodded his head, and smiled. His farm on the outskirts of town had produced an abundant crop this year. The dark, fertile Alabama soil was some of the richest in the state.

Rachel Clair was fifteen, thin, and gawky. She hurried out the front door of the small farmhouse followed closely by her mother, Ada.

"Come straight home after school, Rachel," her mother said. "There'll be no standing around and wasting valuable time with Lolly. We have to start supper early."

"Why is she like that, Daddy? She never lets me do anything," Rachel said as she climbed up on the wagon. "She always makes me come straight home. Lolly's my best friend, and we talk to friends in town after school. That's all."

"Do what she says, she knows best," said Noble.

The Clairs lived in Coal Springs, a farming and rural resort town in the foothills of the Appalachian Mountains in central Alabama. The ride to town was short, and the warm breeze filled the air with dust from the dry dirt road.

"I'll see you tonight, Daddy," she said as her father pulled the reins to stop the old horse.

Rachel grabbed her books and straightened her dress. She then pulled out a comb and hand mirror from her book satchel, adjusted the large, yellow ribbon that held her long, shiny blonde braid, and calmed the stray hairs that loosened around her face.

"Hurry up; we only have a minute until Miss Cates rings the bell," shouted her friend, Lolly Hanes.

"I'm coming."

Rachel was one of twelve girls and eight boys in the schoolhouse. The Coal Springs School consisted of one classroom, and the students ranged in age from six to seventeen. There would be two students graduating this year. Rachel and Lolly were sophomores. Ned McClure and Mattie Boatright were the seniors. The rest of the pupils were younger and in the elementary grades.

"Let's go to the creek this afternoon," Lolly said. "I haven't been in two days."

"I can't. I have to go straight home today. Ada won't let me do anything. I'll be glad when I can argue with her."

"Come on, anyway. She'll never know. It's on the way home," Lolly said. "By the way, why do you always call your mother, Ada?"

"I just like to, okay?" Rachel said with a furrowed brow, then changed the subject. "Maybe I'll go to the creek, maybe not."

Rachel knew why Lolly wanted to go to the creek. She thought Ned McClure was handsome and wanted to follow him after school to Cain Creek where he would swim briefly every afternoon after classes. He never swam very long since he had to work on the family farm. Rachel had tagged along a couple of times and realized Lolly only wanted to watch Ned swim naked. After resisting the thought all day, Rachel decided to go. It was early fall and still warm outside.

Miss Cates rang the school bell at two o'clock. The first student out was Ned McClure. Lolly looked at Rachel with her pleading expression.

Rachel rolled her eyes. "Okay."

Lolly smiled and clapped her hands.

They gave Ned a head start then followed him. He found the dirt path that led to the creek then ducked under a low branch. He'd worn a long trail to a clearing next to the water. The girls were careful not to make any noise.

"I'll die if he hears us," Lolly whispered.

Following in Ned's footsteps, the girls stopped and found a hiding place. They were well hidden and watched him step behind some low brush. He took off his muslin shirt and placed it on top of the bushes, unbuckled his belt, and bent down to unlace his dusty boots. Ned wiped the dirt off and set them on the ground. He dropped his pants along with his long-johns and walked toward the water.

The few times she and Lolly followed Ned, Rachel wouldn't watch. It was too embarrassing. But when the suntanned shoulders and muscular arms were exposed, she couldn't turn away. His perfect physique reminded her of one of the Roman statues in their world history book. She could see only his bare backside, and that was enough. Now she understood why Lolly wanted to follow him.

"Look at him," Lolly said. "Look how he swims. He's sleek, like an eel."

Seeing Ned swim and glide through the water caused a strange and new sensation within her. Rachel wondered about the front of him. She felt herself blush and shook her head to banish the sinful thoughts but couldn't take her eyes off him.

"Lolly, we need to go before Ned gets out."

"No, the good part is when he gets out."

The girls continued to watch Ned swim for a few more minutes, then head to the edge.

"I think he swims to cool off before he has to go home," Lolly said. "That has to be it."

"It's secluded here. Ned probably enjoys the natural springs in the creek and the silence. It's also beautiful," Rachel said. "I bet he comes here to get away from everything and relax; I feel terrible watching him."

"He's about to get out. Wait until you see this," Lolly whispered.

Ned swam to the edge of Cain Creek and stepped onto the bank. His wet, dark brown hair glistened as he shook the water from it. The beads of water caused his tanned skin to shine, and the small amount of dark hair on his chest seemed to cling to each muscle. As Ned lay naked on the bank in the sun, Rachel Clair found herself in the presence of perfection.

CHAPTER 2

SPRING 1907

Rachel couldn't forget that day by the creek. She remembered Ned's gloriously naked body but never thought about the person inside. Almost two years had passed, and the McClures' no longer lived in Coal Springs.

After Ned graduated, Rachel heard through church gossip the McClure family left the area due to foreclosure on "Serenity Farm." Ned's parents rarely socialized but had lived in Coal Springs for more than twenty-five years. Ada always said Leona and Josiah McClure's world consisted of Serenity Farm and Ned. The entire scenario seemed strange to Rachel. She knew Ned as the handsome boy in school, and at Cain Creek, that was all. He was two years older and never paid any attention to her. When he graduated and left the area, she was nothing but a gawky fifteen-year-old.

Now seventeen and about to graduate, Rachel thought about college. Lolly was planning to leave for Howard College in Birmingham and become a teacher. Lolly, a teacher. Really? Lolly had a short attention span, and boys were the only subject that held her interest. Within the last two years Lolly had matured, but not to the extent of being studious and having a teaching career. Her irresponsible best friend skipped school from time to time and sneaked away to the unknown with young transient farmhands that worked on nearby farms.

Rachel knew her father couldn't afford college. Even though she studied hard, her marks weren't good enough for a scholarship. How Lolly got into Howard since her grades were below average was a mystery. Perhaps Dr. Justus Hanes donated money to the Baptist college. Lolly wasn't smart, just rich and spoiled.

Graduation was in three days, and Rachel had no immediate plans. Her father tried his best to work the college funds into the small budget but couldn't cut any more corners. Noble Clair had to take care of his family and the farm. Ada tried to stay positive and teach Rachel how to run a home and be productive. Rachel was learning to cook, and after graduation, she planned to take on some of her mother's burdens.

Lolly and Rachel were the only students graduating. The ceremony was short and attended by close family and friends. Miss Cates awarded the girls their Coal Springs School diplomas and wished them well on their future journeys.

"I can't wait," Lolly began. "In a few months, I'll be at Howard and meeting new people. Aren't you excited for me?"

Before Rachel could answer, Miss Cates placed her arm about her shoulder and walked outside. "Don't worry about not going to college, Rachel. You'll do great things in this world. College isn't all there is to life, you know," she began, "I didn't finish college, and I've been teaching school for ten years."

"Really?" Rachel asked.

"Really. When you understand the fundamentals of teaching and are passionate about it, you can teach others," Miss Cates said. "Find something you love and be good at it. Then you'll be fulfilled."

After the teacher's pep talk, Rachel's entire attitude changed. It was okay that she wasn't going to college. She would discover what her passion in life was in other ways.

Summer, 1907, was coming to an end, and Rachel dreaded the day when Lolly would leave for college. The girls spent every possible moment they could together. Even though boys were able to swim in Cain Creek most of the time, there were a few times during the week, girls were allowed.

"I think it's unfair that we can't swim when we want to," Lolly said as they walked to the creek. "You know the boys always swim naked. Those religious bitches think it's so isolated here, but those church people have no idea. Do they think we don't hide out and watch?"

"Today we're allowed to swim, so let's go and stay until dark," Rachel said. "You go to the creek a lot without me, don't you?"

"I do, but it's not that much fun anymore since Ned McClure moved away," Lolly began, "because it's mostly the Crabtree and Foley boys, and they're not much to see." Lolly shaded her eyes with her hand and squinted in the sun. "Why do we have to wear bathing clothes? The boys aren't required to. I'm taking mine off after we get there."

When they found the familiar branch that marked the path to the creek, Rachel followed Lolly to the overgrown brush where Ned had always shed his clothes.

"Come on, don't wear your swim dress," said Lolly. "The water feels so good next to your bare body."

Rachel was hesitant. "What if someone sees us? Old Mrs. Crabtree would tell everybody in town."

"Old Mrs. Crabtree's nothing to worry about," Lolly began, "she sits at church all day with all the other ladies that think they're holier than God." Lolly started to take her clothes off and spread them on the brush. "Just be glad we're not swimming on Sunday. She'd say we were going straight to hell."

Rachel laughed, but Lolly was right. If they got caught, Lolly was going off to college and Rachel would be left with the town ridicule.

"Come on, take your clothes off and get in," Lolly said as she ran buck naked to the edge of the creek. She waded in and began to swim. "It's warm!"

"Okay." Rachel proceeded to slowly take her clothes off, one piece at a time. She was embarrassed. It's only Lolly. *Do it,*

Rachel. She placed her clothes on a different bush and ran to the water. She waded in and swam out to Lolly.

Lolly screamed with glee, "Aren't you glad your naked? Doesn't it feel wonderful?"

~

After Lolly left for college, Rachel walked the lovely canopied paths by Cain Creek almost daily remembering the days after school when she and her best friend had watched Ned McClure swim in the nude. That was a vision she would never forget.

The Alabama autumns stayed warm until October. With Coal Springs School back in session, Rachel found time to swim every day in the creek. She loved the peaceful feeling of the warm spring water on her nude body. She learned to glide through the water and never cause a ripple, just like Ned.

Rachel and Lolly corresponded regularly, and it seemed as if her friend did nothing but go to parties at Howard. One letter described college life through Lolly's eyes:

October 1, 1907
My dearest friend,

Oh, how you would love this place. I've met many students yet haven't found anyone like you. The girls are nice but too severe. The boys are attentive, and I seem to have an engagement with a different one each night. The weekend parties are fun, but with this a Baptist institution, there isn't much dancing or music. There are clubs here called fraternities for the boys and sororities for the girls. Oh, dear friend, how I miss you.
Lolly

Reading Lolly's letters made Rachel feel envious. If she had a chance to go to college, it would be to learn and make her life mean something. Now she helped her mother clean, cook, and sew. She wanted much more than this.

"Rachel, take your father his lunch," Ada said. "He should be in the Number nine apple orchard by now."

Noble Clair owned twelve acres and grew cotton, apples, pears, and a variety of vegetables. Rachel and Ada canned the produce throughout the summer so there would be plenty for the winter.

The Number nine apple orchard was ten minutes from the house, on foot. As she approached it, Rachel could hear the jingle of Old General's harness while he shook off the flies. The old horse stood attached to the wagon in the shade of one of the ten apple trees. Noble and a new farmhand, holding sturdy sticks, were hitting the lower limbs of another tree to loosen the fruit.

"Daddy, lunch," shouted Rachel. She hoped there was enough for the farmhand.

Noble and the man stopped and threw down their sticks. Rachel noticed the farmhand was young, but that was all. She sat on the back of the wagon and laid out the lunch Ada had prepared.

As the men approached, Rachel squinted to get a good look at the farmhand.

"Ned, you remember my daughter, Rachel, from school, don't you?"

"Sure, I do. It's been a few years, though," he said.

The wide brim of the hand's weather-worn hat covered his face. When he removed it, Rachel couldn't believe it; Ned McClure. All she could think about was his beautiful, naked body. He must be nineteen or twenty by now.

"Hello, Ned. We haven't seen you around since your family moved away. Are you back in town for good?"

"I hope so. It all depends on how much work I can get. Coal Springs is my home. I remember it being quiet and peaceful. I especially liked to swim in Cain Creek," he said.

His natural good looks were the same, but his personality seemed much friendlier. Rachel remembered him as one who never spoke to anyone and stayed to himself. Had he changed in that regard or was he being cordial because of Noble?

Since there was plenty of food, Rachel stayed and had lunch with the two men. The subject was nothing but the apple crop and how fast it had to be harvested and taken to market. Noble treated his farmhands well, and Rachel hoped Ned would stay a while. She was curious, however, about how and where he had spent the past two years of his life.

Ned had a vague memory of Rachel, but she looked different. He remembered her as a freckled-faced gawky girl with big teeth. Her face had matured, the braid she always wore was gone, and her long, blonde wavy hair fell freely about her shoulders. She had grown into a beautiful young lady.

Ned had paid no attention to Rachel while at Coal Springs School, but he was now. During lunch, and listening to Noble discuss the harvest, Ned studied her face. Under her large straw hat, he noticed her brown eyes, straight nose, and perfectly shaped lips. She had a small, slim figure which enhanced the light blue day dress. While Rachel served the sandwiches, he noticed her pretty hands and liked how she smiled when he thanked her for such a nice lunch.

Her cheeks blushed. "My mother prepared it," she said.

After a full day's work, the two men loaded the buckboard and Old General turned in the direction of the barn. After the bushels were unloaded, Ned headed to the bunkhouse.

"Ned, come on up to the house for supper about six," said Noble. "Two other farmhands arrive in the morning, and I can't play favorites after tonight."

"I'm grateful, Mr. Clair. I'll be there."

On the way to the bunkhouse, Ned thought about his parents with sadness. Almost two years had passed since they died.

In the summer of 1905, Ned and his family had moved to Birmingham after his graduation from Coal Springs School. His future college plans were put on hold when his father was notified of Serenity Farm's foreclosure due to non-payment of the mortgage. His father had become ill with consumption that year. The disease caused a robust and strong Josiah McClure to weaken into a frail, bedridden man. Ned took over the crops and chores of Serenity Farm for his father, but he and his mother, Leona, couldn't do it alone. His father remained adamant about the importance of Ned's education.

"I'd rather lose the crops than you lose your education, Son," his father would say.

Ned's father lost his crops and their beloved family farm. Soon after the notification of foreclosure, the formal notice of eviction was issued.

The devout citizens of Coal Springs smirked, pointed, and called his mother terrible names as the McClure family left with only the possessions packed and crowded on their wagon. Weren't these people supposed to offer a shoulder to lean on; give unsolicited help to ones in need? As Ned and his parents rode out of Coal Springs in disgrace, he never forgot the words on a sign the members of the church erected:

"Welcome to Coal Springs.
We are All One Family in God."

Josiah and Leona McClure were given nothing in the way of friendship or assistance. That day of cruel scrutiny toward his parents marked the last time Ned McClure stepped inside a church.

The one-story farmhouse had been built on land handed down to each generation of Clairs since the Alabama pioneers settled in the area in 1829. The house sat at the end of a long, dirt drive canopied with oak trees. It was built in 1856 after the original log house was destroyed by fire. The front porch enabled the small house to appear large from a distance, and brick chimneys flanked each side.

Noble Clair was the fourth generation and like his father, took pride in his farm and reaped the rewards of his hard work. He was careful when he hired farmhands to work the fields, and if he was crossed by one, they were dismissed. Many farmhands had come and gone through the years. Transient farm labor was hired in September for the fall harvest, and rarely did they work on the same farm twice. If they did, it was at the landowner's request.

Noble dropped Ned at the bunkhouse; then let Old General find his way to the barn. He unharnessed Old General, followed the horse to his stall, and cushioned it with fresh hay. As his old friend drank water from the trough, Noble added grain to the feeding bucket and latched the stall door.

"Goodnight, old friend."

The cool nights were approaching, and Noble noticed smoke rising from one of the house chimneys. His thoughts instantly turned to the first fire of the season. All summer, he had longed to sit in his rocking chair on a cool night while feeling its warmth and taking in the enticing odor of hickory.

"I've invited Ned for supper. He'll be here at six," called Noble. He removed his hat and work boots and sat in his old rocker in front of the fire. Hiring Ned was a good decision. The boy was strong, decent, and his parents were good people. He never understood why the McClures were run out of town and refused to listen to the constant gossip from the ladies of the church.

Rachel walked into the parlor stroking the head of a small grey cat.

"We have an extra for supper tonight, Rachel," called Ada. "Go ahead, set the table, and make sure you put Christobel out. That cat hisses at every person who darkens the door."

Rachel refused to put Christobel outside. She loved the sweet creature and was frightened a predator would attack her. Christobel always stayed inside. She was skittish around everyone but Rachel and her father. Two years before, Noble found the kitten crouched in the corner of Old General's stall after a thunderstorm and gave her to his daughter to care for. She would leave her in the bedroom and close the door.

There was a loud knock at the front door at six o'clock. Rachel had no idea who the extra place at the table was for since her father never had farmhands to the house.

"Hello, Rachel," said Ned as he removed his hat. "Your father invited me to supper."

"I'm glad. Come in." A blush heated Rachel's cheeks. The only guests they ever had were stodgy Reverend Bradshaw and a few self-righteous deacons and their wives from the church. They came for lunch after services on Sundays and spoke about nothing but gossip and sin.

"It smells good in here," said Ned. "It reminds me of my mother's kitchen."

"Where do your parents live now?" Rachel asked. "Did you travel very far—"

Noble loudly cleared his throat as he got up to shake Ned's hand. "Glad to see you, boy. Starting tomorrow, we have a lot of work to do, and we need to make sure you have plenty of energy."

Ned smiled at Rachel and turned to Noble. "Like I was saying to Rachel, this house brings back a lot of good memories for me."

Rachel waited for Ned to answer her question about his parents. The subject didn't come up again. Ada motioned to Rachel for assistance, so Noble offered Ned a small glass of scotch. Afraid Christobel might appear, Rachel looked toward her bedroom and noticed the door ajar but shrugged and joined her mother. The table was laden with a variety of fresh vegetables and roast beef. The men and Ada sat first, then Rachel. When Noble said grace, Rachel looked at Ned. His eyes remained open, and he didn't bow his head. Then the full bowls were passed, plates were piled high, and the only sound was the tinkling of drinking glasses and utensils touching porcelain plates.

"The new hands will be arriving early in the morning," Noble said. "Old Crabtree at the mercantile is putting them up tonight and will carry them out here around seven. Ned, I'd like you to be out there with me when they get here."

"Yes, sir. I will."

"There should be three of them, I believe," Noble began, then looked at Ada, "and they shouldn't need anything in the way of food until lunch."

"I'll have breakfast ready at six-thirty, Ned."

Christobel jumped into Rachel's lap. Ned reached over to pet her, and the small cat leaned in and rubbed her head into the palm of his hand.

"Rachel, I told you to put that cat out."

"She isn't hissing. She likes Ned," said Rachel as she handed the cat to Ned.

Ned continued to stroke Christobel's head as she lay down in his lap and began to purr.

Rachel came into the parlor where Noble was sound asleep in his old worn chair in front of the fire. Ned walked around the room, looking at family photographs as he continued to hold the sleeping feline.

"She likes you," Rachel said. "She usually likes only Daddy and me. She hisses at everybody."

"I like cats. We used to have an old tabby named Yellow Tim," Ned said. "He died a few years ago at the ripe old age of seventeen. Here, take her." Ned handed the cat to Rachel. "I need to be going. I won't disturb Noble. I already thanked your mother."

"I guess I'll see you at lunch tomorrow," said Rachel.

Ned looked at Rachel and smiled. "Goodnight," he said as he put on his weather-worn hat and walked out the door into the darkness.

CHAPTER 3

NEW ARRIVALS

Fall 1907

Ned and Noble waited in front of the farmhand's cabin for Old Crabtree's wagon. At seven o'clock, the muffled clip-clop of a small team of horses could be heard down the dirt drive. As the buckboard pulled in front of the cabin, Ned saw three men riding in the back. All three were young white men looking to be in their early twenties.

"Welcome men," said Noble. "We have a lot to harvest so drop your gear in the bunkhouse and let's get started."

Old Crabtree gave Noble a slip of paper with each man's name and information. Two had a permanent address, while one only mentioned his home state.

"Which one is Wiley Lovett?" asked Noble.

"Me, sir," said one of the men.

"Hewlitt Griffin?"

"That would be me, sir," replied the young man with blond hair.

"You have to be James Cason," said Noble.

As Noble looked over the farmhand's papers, he read that Hewlitt Griffin was the youngest of the three at age eighteen. He lived in Branchville and graduated from high school in the spring. He postponed college until January and planned to major in agriculture but wanted to get hands-on experience at a working farm. Wiley Lovett, from Riverton, was twenty and married. He had one child and worked as a transient farmhand during each seasonal Alabama harvest.

As Noble read James Cason's information, he picked his teeth with his ever-present silver toothpick and spat while sensing an air about him that didn't mesh with the others.

"You look familiar. You've worked this area before, right, boy?"

"Yes, sir," said James. "I worked Smalley's place last year, and old man Jonas's the year before." His papers documented his age as twenty-five, from Tupelo, Mississippi, and unmarried. He was nice looking, in a seedy sort of way, but seemed cocky and indifferent.

"You ready to work, boy?" Noble asked.

"Yes, sir," James answered. "I'm ready. Just say the word." He looked around as he wiped his nose with the back of his hand.

Ned led Old General and the buckboard out of the barn to the bunkhouse. Noble and the new hands climbed on the wagon as Ned took the reins.

Rachel woke up to Christobel, kneading her claws in her blanket. She grabbed the cat and pulled her close. "Come here, sweet girl. You and I don't have to get up yet."

When she pulled up the covers, the cat went underneath and lay next to her. Rachel loved how her sweet companion's cuddlesome body kept her warm. She slept for another hour and missed breakfast. Now she would have to get up and help prepare the lunches. She didn't like meeting new hands. There had been men in the past who had eyed her with lust, and it made her uncomfortable.

Rachel's small bedroom was bright and consisted of a small iron bed, a heavy rocker upholstered in a Victorian rose pattern, and a tall wooden mirror attached to a matching dressing table. A nightstand held a pure white porcelain bowl and matching pitcher for washing, and a large chifforobe stood in one corner. After splashing cold water on her face, Rachel pulled out a day outfit of a white embroidered blouse and ankle-length black skirt. Sitting on a stool at her dressing table, she brushed her long hair one hundred strokes then pulled it back into a loose, low chignon.

Ada packed the lunches and gave the basket to Rachel to deliver to the Number two orchard. She put the filled basket on her arm and started the ten-minute walk. She was glad autumn had finally arrived. It seemed as if the trees were swaying happily in the cool breeze. Soon the leaves would change, and the farm would be painted in vibrant colors of orange, red, and yellow. Rachel thought she might have discovered her passion. Nature. She loved every aspect of it, but how could she learn the fundamental principles of it without going to college? The closest library was in Oden, which was almost eight miles away on good roads. She would have to put her passion aside a little while longer.

As she approached the orchard, Rachel could hear Old General shaking his head and then the sound of young male voices. As always, she spread out the lunch on the back of the buckboard for the farmhands and her father.

"Who's that ripe apple waiting to be picked?" asked James. "I could easily bite off a piece of that."

"Be careful, that's Mr. Clair's daughter," said Ned. "Don't let me hear anything inappropriate about her from you."

"Such a big word coming from you. Got a thing for her, do ya?" James asked.

"No, but she's a nice girl, and I'd hate to know you'd cheapened her in some way."

"Don't worry. I won't tell you if I do," James said with a smirk.

Ned grabbed his shirt and brought James's face close to his. "You touch her or say anything about her you couldn't say in front of your mother; I'll make sure you're out of here. You understand?"

James pushed Ned's hand away. "Take her for yourself; you know you want to."

Rachel called Noble and the hands over to the wagon for lunch.

ꝏ

Ned watched Rachel walk away from the orchard. Maybe James is right, and I do want her for myself. James and his sordid remarks caused Ned to re-evaluate his position at the Clair farm. He was a farmhand like the others but felt the need to protect Rachel from James and his sort. Ned wanted no problems, so he planned to keep his distance from James, even though it would be difficult.

When the men took their break for lunch, Ned grabbed his portion and headed for the shade under one of the large apple trees. On the wagon, a bucket with a ladle held fresh spring water, and Ned filled his tin cup. Wiley joined him, but neither spoke a word.

Rachel returned to retrieve the lunch basket, and Ned watched James stop what he was doing then whisper something about her to Hewlitt and laugh.

"Daddy, I brought some baked cookies for you and the men," Rachel called out. "I'll see you later."

As Ned eyed James, his hand balled into a tight fist, then loosened it. James wasn't worth the time or effort. He returned to the orchard and filled basket after basket until he heard Noble call out the words he was waiting to hear.

"Okay, men, let's call it quits for the day," Noble placed his overflowing basket of apples on the back of the wagon. "You boys bring in your pickins,' and we'll be heading back to the house."

The sun cast long shadows as it painted the sky. It was setting early now. Ned could see that Noble was pleased with the twenty-five large baskets full of Red Delicious apples.

“You men have worked hard today,” he said. “Ned, you drive the wagon.”

Ned was dirty, sweaty, and his clothes stunk. As he guided Old General back to the barn, he decided on a swim in Cain Creek. The water would be cold, but he didn’t care. That was his favorite place on earth since he could be alone and push his bad memories aside for a short time. He hadn’t been there in two years. It had only been two days since he’d come back to Coal Springs.

After the wagon was unloaded, Noble guided Old General to his stall. Ned took his leave and headed to the creek. It was dusk, but he had enough daylight for a quick swim. He found the familiar low branch he once used as a marker to find his path. Some of the brush was overgrown but not much. It looked as if someone walked the trail regularly. He followed the imprint of small bare feet past the bushes where he used to shed his clothes. The footprints stopped at the large clearing next to the creek. Ned saw no one and heard no one as he removed his work clothes. The chill in the air felt exhilarating, and he sprinted to the water and dove in. The creek was warm from the natural springs, and after the ripple from the dive calmed, he glided through the water, barely making a sound. As he raised his head out of the water for a breath, he heard rustling.

“Anyone there?” There was no answer. “Hello?” He shrugged, swam to the bank, and got out. Nothing but some varmint. He shivered in the cool temperature.

~

“Rachel Clair, where are you?” Ada called out the screened door of the main house. “It’s time to take supper to the men, and she’s nowhere to be found,” she mumbled to herself.

After a few minutes, Rachel opened the door. “Sorry, Ada, I took a short walk. Time to take food to the farmhands?”

"Why do you continue to call me Ada?" she said with irritation. "With four men to feed, it'll take both of us, and we'll need the large pushcart."

Rachel went back outside and met Ned walking in front of the main house on his way back to the bunkhouse. Butterflies filled her stomach. She hoped he hadn't seen her hiding in the bushes by the creek. She noticed his hair was still wet and how his damp shirt clung to his muscular chest. "Supper's ready. We'll be over there soon," she said as Ned tipped his hat and smiled. She began to walk with him. "Have you seen the large pushcart in the barn?" Rachel asked.

"No, but I'll try to find it."

She accompanied him into the barn, and after moving a few bales of hay and Old General's wagon, Ned found it wedged between the plow and the slat wall of the barn.

"Stand clear; I'll need a little room to pry this thing out," he said. After a few minutes, Ned had freed the large cart and maneuvered it out the large barn door.

"Thank you. Why is your hair wet?"

"Oh, I went for a swim in Cain Creek. I used to swim there a lot when I lived here. Do you ever swim there?"

"Yes, but only on ladies' allowed days, though." Rachel didn't mention the times she swam alone.

"I remember that nonsense," Ned said as he smiled. "I'll see you in a bit."

Rachel turned her head as her face had blushed blood red. *Why do I feel so odd when he's close to me?* Seeing him swim again brought out unfamiliar wants and needs within her. She wondered how it would feel to kiss his lips or to experience his embrace. She felt safe with him.

Rachel cleaned up the pushcart and covered it with a cotton tablecloth. Ada filled it with a cast-iron cauldron full of beef stew, cornbread, fresh milk, baked apples, and a pot of coffee. Before entering the bunkhouse, she and Ada filled each plate and carried them to the small table for four in the cabin. The cabin was old but had a large fireplace for heat and four beds for the hands. There wasn't much room for anything else.

"This smells good, Mrs. Clair," said James. "I'm starved." He looked at Rachel and smiled. "Did you help, Miss Rachel?"

Rachel blushed. "Yes, I did. I made the baked apples, and I hope you all like them."

"I'm sure we will," James said as his eyes combed every inch of Rachel's body. "They look firm and sweet."

Rachel saw Ned shoot a glance at James, accompanied by a furrowed brow. *Why did he do that?* She thought the comment from James was a compliment to her cooking.

The women returned within the hour for the dishes. As Rachel scraped the plates and placed them in a basket, James remained at the table.

"Thank you for a delicious meal, Mrs. Clair. You too, Miss Rachel." James called to them as they left the cabin.

"I think James is nice, don't you?" Rachel remarked to Ada while they pushed the large cart back to the house. "He's nothing like Ned, though. Ned's gentle and sincere; not brash like James." She tightened the lightweight shawl around her arms. The temperature seemed to be dropping.

Ada remained silent. After a moment, she remarked, "I wouldn't trust James with a wild bobcat. He'd sweet-talk the poor animal into its own grave--alive."

Ned poured a stiff whiskey and took advantage of the cool evening. He walked to the barn and checked on Old General, then sat on a log he planned to bust up for firewood. He looked over at the main house and saw Rachel through the kitchen window, helping her mother. She was beautiful, sweet, and genuine. There wasn't an ounce of falseness about her. He watched through the window until the light went out.

As Ned continued to sip his drink, a small figure came out from the shadows.

"Enjoying the night air?" Rachel asked.

"I am, what about you? Taking a walk?"

"I thought I might. Would you like to join me?"

Ned set his glass on the log. "Love to."

Rachel smelled of hickory and lilacs. He liked the way her blonde hair fell freely about her shoulders and that her beauty wasn't concealed in any way. Her lips were naturally pink, and the thickness of her eyelashes seemed to line her brown eyes. He found himself staring.

"Do you usually take a walk at night?" he asked.

"Not really. I'll confess, I saw you sitting on the log."

Ned smiled. "We should do this every night. How 'bout it?"

"Sure. I'd like that." Rachel looked at him and timidly smiled. "Let's walk to the road and back. My mother will start looking for me in about five minutes."

As they walked, Rachel told him what Miss Cates had said about college and how she planned to study nature when her father could find a way to afford it.

"I can see you as a plant scientist. Nature abounds around here," he said as he looked around, then up to the clear, dark sky. "Look at all the stars. Have you ever seen anything so fascinating? That twinkling red one is Mars, I think."

"I see the Big Dipper." Rachel pointed to it. "Find it?"

Ned got a little closer and followed her finger to get her view of it. "I see it now."

As Rachel put her arm down, he realized his face was next to hers. She turned to him, and he gently kissed her.

CHAPTER 4

THE HARVEST DANCE

October marked the end of the 1907 fall harvest. Ned heard nothing else out of James about Rachel. The four men ended up working well together and helped Noble bring in a bountiful crop. The Clair farm produced quality fruits and vegetables, so Noble was able to ask and get top dollar for it.

Rachel realized the farmhands would be moving on in a week, and she hated to see Ned leave. She liked him and his natural good looks. He was gentle and kind but seemed preoccupied. He kept to himself, and never socialized with the other men. That was the mysterious Ned McClure she remembered from school, and this intrigued her. This Ned seemed to hide behind a shield of protection. She and the friendly Ned had formed a sort of bond, and he seemed relaxed with her. They continued their nightly walks, even though she had to sneak out of the house.

Even though Rachel thought James Cason lazy, he was ruggedly attractive and cordial to her. He often brought her a bouquet of wildflowers that grew on the hill across from Cain Creek. James had asked her to walk with him many times, but she knew her mother didn't like him and found an excuse to decline the invitation. However, Rachel decided to be through with pleasing her mother. Ada was just like those church women; too devout and proper for her own good. The next time James asked, she would accept whether her mother approved or not.

A community dance and dinner had been planned for all departing transient farmhands. The event would be held in the

Pavilion at the Mountain Lodge Hotel in appreciation for their hard work.

Almost eighteen, Rachel was excited. The dance would be her first since the farmhands this year were friends and didn't make her feel uncomfortable. Rachel was a natural beauty, and her flawless skin and dark eyes illuminated her loose flowing blonde hair. For the dance, she would pin it up like the "Gibson" girls in the magazines and wear her light blue chiffon and lace satin ankle-length dress. She pinched her cheeks for a rosy blush after securing the pompadour chignon with the last hairpin. There was a vessel full of wildflowers on the dining room table. "Ada, will you secure these flowers in my hair?"

As Ada entered the dining room, she gasped and brought her hands to her cheeks. "Rachel, you look beautiful. I can't wait until your father sees you," she said. After dotting the flowers around the loose chignon, she said, "Wait here."

In a few minutes, Ada returned with a small jewelry box. Inside were a pair of ivory satin gloves, a long strand of pearls, and matching pearl earrings. "These should look just right with your dress."

While Ada helped with the gloves and tightened the pearl earrings to her ears, Rachel looked at her image in the mirror and liked what she saw. She smiled at the reflection of the once awkward adolescent girl that had grown into a beauty.

"You're a young woman now. You should look the part," said Ada while adjusting the long pearls to the correct length.

After returning to Coal Springs, Ned had passed his parent's beloved Serenity Farm on a few occasions but never stopped. He intentionally stayed away since there were too many memories, good and bad, associated with the farm. Now that the harvest was over, he planned to open the old gate and revisit the only home he ever knew. His parents had made it a happy place, a loving place, a warm place. He would make his appearance at the fall dance that night, but now he was going to Serenity Farm.

Ned walked the ten minutes from the Clair farm and approached the old iron gate. The white paint had chipped off in places, but the strong rusty hinges still held up. He smiled when he removed the rusted old padlock and heard the all too familiar creak when it opened. The old azalea and camellia bushes hadn't changed, but his mother's flower garden and the well were covered with weeds and old kudzu vines. The sign, Serenity Farm, still hung on the porch but dangled on one hook. Old wisteria vines clung to the roof and one side of the house.

He walked the property and found the once productive fields overgrown with weeds. The aging white two-story house was in disrepair, and the wooden steps to the front porch were rotten. Families of chipmunks and other rodents lived underneath. The screened door was ajar, and the front door was unlocked. Ned walked into a house that was filthy and uninhabitable. The old structure was empty except for a few old wooden chairs and a couple of dusty crates scattered about the parlor. "Damned vagrants," Ned mumbled as he found burned out candles and whiskey bottles. The stairs to the second floor were rotten in places, so he had to hold tight to the railing as he made his way up. There were broken out windows in his parent's old bedroom upstairs and busted walls in his. Ned walked back into his parent's bedroom to see if there was one tiny fragment of his parents remaining in there. He hoped to find anything that could've been missed from the sell-off.

He opened the door of an old built-in cabinet where his mother kept her cherished possessions. Ned looked around the inside of the cabinet and noticed a loose piece of wood and pulled it out. He found an old velvet box tied with faded satin ribbon. He opened it to see a thin, yellowed folded note. Ned looked up, closed his eyes, and let out a deep breath. He held on to the paper but placed the box back where he found it.

Addressed to his mother, Leona, Ned opened it to find a short note:

My dearest darling, I miss you so. How hard it was to see you
at the Pavilion tonight. You were with Josiah and seeing
him touch you sent daggers through my heart. I know we
must be careful since our baby will be born soon.
Even if we can't speak in public, all I need is a loving glance from you.
Your servant always, L

There was no date, and the script was unfamiliar. *What baby? Did his mother have another child? What happened to it? Who is "L"? Was she having an affair with some man here in town?* Ned's thoughts were uncontrolled as he continued to search the secret compartment. He pushed his hand as far back in the small space as it could go but found nothing else. His parents were kind, loving, and spiritual. What could have driven his mother to adultery? Ned folded the yellowed note and placed it in his pocket, then went downstairs. He left his beloved Serenity Farm saddened, confused, and wanting answers.

Ned's plan all along had been to return to Coal Springs and one day buy back the farm. He wanted to bring the fallow fields back to life, and the desire to live there again had been utmost for his future plans. But now, seeing it in this deplorable condition and realizing the obvious lie his parents lived, how could he repair the damage to himself or the farm?

∞

Rachel came into the parlor where her parents were waiting. "You are just beautiful, Rachel," her father praised as he placed a pink chiffon shawl about her shoulders. "My little girl has grown up."

They arrived at the large clearing close to the railroad trestle. Noble guided Old General to the area where horses and wagons were kept during all Pavilion activities. Rachel pinched her cheeks again.

"I'm nervous. What if no one asks me to dance?" Rachel asked as Noble helped her off the wagon.

"I don't think you'll have to worry about that," Ada said with a proud smile.

The tall trestle bridge connected the railroad platform to the hotel, and as the Clair's approached it, a loud voice was heard in the distance.

"Rachel! Wait for me!" James Cason ran to catch up.

She noticed Ada's furrowed brow, and her mother's comment was inaudible.

"Hello, James, old boy," said Noble as he shook the boy's hand. "Glad to see you."

"I wouldn't miss this, Mr. Clair," he said. "Rachel, save some dances for me, all right?"

Rachel grinned. She noticed his rugged good looks and how his usual disheveled appearance was gone, replaced with combed hair and scented pomade. His dark pin-striped suit was pressed, and he wore a small flower in his lapel.

His eyes brightened. "For you." James presented Rachel a small wildflower bouquet bound with pale pink ribbons.

"Thank you," Rachel said as she nodded her head with gratitude.

James joined the Clairs as they walked to the Pavilion. Presenting their tickets to old Mrs. Crabtree, they entered the large, open room. Rachel was excited to hear the Fontainbleu Orchestra. The couples danced the two-step, and she was thankful her father had taught her that one. Now, she wouldn't embarrass herself, too much.

"Come on, Rachel," James said with excitement, "let's dance."

The orchestra played, and Rachel handed her shawl to Ada as James took her hand.

"You look beautiful," James whispered.

Rachel timidly looked up into his brown eyes and smiled. *Please don't let me step on his feet.*

As the music played, James placed his hand firmly around her waist and took her left hand. Rachel remembered the book Lolly gave her on etiquette and how to conduct herself when dancing. When James pulled her closer, she stiffened. Rachel noticed the other couples dancing just as close. She liked his strong arm around her and tightened her arm about his neck. That gesture caused James to pull her even closer.

Looking around the room, Rachel noticed the line of church women watching them with smirks denoting disapproval and nodding their heads in agreement. Mrs. Foley, her spinster daughter Janette, and Mrs. Pope were friends of Ada's and the worst gossip mongers in town. They would no doubt report their dim view of her illicit behavior to her father. Rachel didn't care since she'd done nothing wrong. She was having the time of her life.

"Enjoying yourself?" James asked. "You dance well."

She looked into his blue eyes and smiled. "Yes, very much."

From the first day on the Clair farm, James's thoughts of Rachel consumed him. Now he had her in his arms. She acted innocent and inexperienced, but he could tell she was ripe and ready for him. If only he could get her alone.

James was surprised at how good this beautiful girl felt in his arms. The dance was a two-step, and there wasn't much space between them. Her body felt warm, and her quick side glances seemed to convey anything but shyness and immaturity.

"Ready for a cold drink, Rachel?

She nodded as he guided her off the floor with his hand about her waist. He found a small unoccupied table and pulled out a chair for her.

"Sit here. I'll be right back," James said. "It looks like the entire community is here tonight."

"Yes, unfortunately," Rachel said as he took her hand, squeezed it, and laughed.

The Mountain Lodge Hotel staff used fresh fall leaves and pumpkins from nearby farms for decorations. There was a variety of finger foods and desserts as well as numerous virgin punch bowls covering the main refreshment table. Another table in a shed outside held several washtubs full of spiked concoctions and moonshine.

"Rachel, there you are." It was Lolly Hanes. "I finally found you. Did you receive my last letter telling you I'd be home today?"

"No, I didn't." Rachel jumped up eagerly and hugged her friend. "I'm so happy you're home. When did you mail it?"

"I wrote it the first part of the week, but I probably forgot to mail it," she said. "No matter, I'm home now."

James returned to the table with plates of refreshments and three glasses of punch. Rachel introduced Lolly to him, and he pulled up a chair for her to join them.

"I've missed you so much," Lolly said. "College is great, but I'd rather be here. I can't seem to make many friends there. I'm leaving Howard and coming home after this semester."

"I'm glad. It's so quiet and dull when you're not here," said Rachel.

"Punch?" asked James as Lolly settled in her chair.

"Only if it's spiked," Lolly said with a flirtatious giggle.

"It is, so take it slow," James winked at Rachel.

The six months away at college hadn't changed Lolly. Still the vivacious flirt, there were no holds barred when it came to having fun. Lolly had grown into a statuesque beauty with her wavy dark brown hair and blue eyes. Her low-cut pink chiffon dress was one Rachel hadn't seen, and she was a vision with her long hair piled loosely on top of her head. The stunning simple diamond necklace Lolly wore sparkled as the matching bracelet accented her long white evening gloves. Rachel felt plain sitting next to her.

"Dance, Lolly?" James asked.

"Of course."

Rachel sat alone at the table and noticed Ned McClure entering the Pavilion. He looked good in his dark grey three-piece suit and hordes of butterflies filled her stomach. She watched him as he timidly shook hands and greeted familiar old neighbors. Ned sat down at Ada and Noble's table. He looked uncomfortable, so she left the small table to join her parents. There was one chair available, and it was next to Ned. Taking a deep breath, Rachel smiled and sat down.

"Not dancing, Rachel?" Noble asked as he and Ned stood.

"I was, but James is dancing with Lolly now."

Ned sat down. "Did you come with James tonight?" He seemed disappointed.

"No, he walked in with us. We've only danced one dance."

Rachel caught Ned smiling out of the corner of her eye while he loosened his tie a little.

"I'm not much of a dancer, but would you give me the honor of the next one?" Ned asked.

"I'd love to." Her butterflies were multiplying.

"We saw Lolly come in. Is she home for good? I heard she wasn't going back to Howard," Ada said.

Rachel replied, "Not yet. She won't be home until Christmas, I think."

Lolly's loud laughter was heard as she and James danced by the table. A bit tipsy, Lolly began to stumble, and Rachel thought James was holding her too close.

"That girl is underage. We need to find out who gave her alcohol," said Noble.

"Daddy, she got it herself. It's none of your business."

"Rachel," Ada reacted with the jerk of her head. "Were you addressing your father with that sassy tone?"

"I'm sorry, Daddy," she said. "You know Lolly; she does anything she wants, especially when her father isn't around."

When the dance was over, Rachel watched James leave Lolly at the smaller table and adjust his suit. He walked toward her as the next dance began.

"How 'bout another dance, Rachel?"

"This one is mine, James. Wait your turn," said Ned.

"Sure thing." James backed away and found another partner.

Ned pulled Rachel's chair out and took her hand. His gentle touch sent a tingle down her spine. A slow waltz played.

"I don't know the waltz," she said with hesitation.

"Don't worry; just follow me."

Ned made it easy for her to follow him. He led her around the floor with simple steps while holding her in his strong arms. As her heart raced, she almost melted in his gentle embrace. Rachel looked up and noticed his smile. She blushed as she felt the firm muscles under his sleeve.

"You're doing great," Ned said.

"When did you learn to dance?" Rachel asked as she placed her hand around his neck. She looked for Mrs. Foley, but she had her eye on someone else.

"I used to waltz with my mother from time to time," he said. "She thought I needed to learn since I was getting older. My parents loved to dance."

Rachel didn't want the dance to end. Ned's handsome face was inches from hers, and his embrace made her feel safe and secure. She wanted to kiss him, but that gesture would probably have her run out of town.

After the waltz, Rachel felt as if her cheeks were still blushing. Ned led her back to the table where James waited for her.

"Care to take a walk, Rachel?" James asked.

"I don't know," she said, hoping Ned would intervene. "It is a little stuffy in here." Rachel noticed her mother's familiar disapproving twitch. "I probably shouldn't."

"Is it all right, Mr. Clair?" asked James.

"I guess so, but don't venture away from the Pavilion."

"Ned, would you like to join us?" Rachel asked.

"I appreciate the offer, but I'll stay here," he said.

Disappointed, Rachel looked back at her mother as Ada glared at James. She could almost read her mother's lips as she argued with her father. Ada was angry because Noble had given his permission.

She wanted to venture away from the Pavilion and get away from the same old scowls and raised eyebrows from the old pillars of the church. They didn't approve of a young couple walking without a chaperone. Tonight, she wanted to experience something new and exciting.

James walked her out into the night air and stopped. "Do you think your father would mind if we walked to the hotel?"

"It's closed for the season, but I don't mind."

"As many times as I've worked in this area, I've never been inside the hotel or the cottages. Are there fifteen of them on the grounds?" James asked.

"Yes, and a swimming pool, and a tennis court..."

"Are you cold?" James asked as he noticed her shivering.

"A little," she replied. James took off his jacket and wrapped it around her shoulders.

Even though they could see their way, some of the moonlight was blocked by large tree branches and the nearby cottages. They approached the two-story hotel, and James tried each exterior door to gain access inside. It was no use. The hotel was locked up until June.

"I'm curious about the cottages. Have you ever been in one?" James asked.

"No, but I heard they're cozy. Sometimes they rent out for the entire summer," Rachel said as she pulled the jacket tighter around her shoulders.

Rachel shivered as James tried each cabin door until he found one unlocked. He opened the door of Cabin Number nine and escorted her inside. Finding a kerosene lamp on a small table, he felt for a match in his pocket. The flame cast a soft light in the small room.

"This is nice," Rachel said. The room consisted of a stone fireplace, bed, dresser, and a couple of chairs. Wide planked wood floors were covered with braided throw rugs, and the walls were constructed of knotty pine. Framed pictures of the hotel and a mirror hung on the walls. A tall wooden table with a porcelain washbasin and pitcher stood next to the bed. The cabin seemed quite cozy.

"I agree," James said as he placed the lamp on the table.

"Maybe we should light a fire."

"No! We aren't supposed to be here," Rachel said with a shaky voice.

"You're right. It's too bad, though. It would've created a romantic atmosphere," James said as he locked the cabin door.

Rachel stood in the small cabin and continued to shiver. As she pulled his jacket closer, James walked toward her. She wondered if he would kiss her.

"You're beautiful," James said as he looked into her brown eyes. He bent down and softly kissed her. She didn't turn away or act frightened. "I've wanted to do that for a long time."

"I wanted you to," she said as she headed for the door. She remembered the etiquette book. One kiss, then it's time to say goodnight.

"Wait. Not yet." James took her hand and kept her from the door.

He gently kissed her again. Rachel trembled as he pulled her closer and kissed her face, neck, then found her lips again.

Rachel was feeling excited and aroused. His kisses were causing a strange desire, and she wanted more.

As James continued to kiss her, his hands wandered her body. The kissing was nice, but now he was invading her privacy.

"Stop, James," she said as he held her in a way that almost scared her.

"No, I want you so much," he said as he grabbed her hair and continued to kiss her shoulders and her exposed cleavage. He felt for the buttons of her dress and began to unbutton each one slowly.

She wiggled away and started for the door. James stopped her with one hand on the door, and the other around her waist. He kissed her again, but it was sloppy and rough. Rachel pulled her face away. She noticed his tie was loosened and his pants were unbuttoned. He kept his hand on the door and dropped his pants to the floor.

"Don't, please, James, I'm not like that."

"What are you like? I can satisfy you in every way," he said through heavy breaths.

James pulled her to him, and she felt his bulge against her. He led her to the bed and continued to unbutton the dress. He stopped and kissed her gently.

"I can see you like tenderness," he said. "I'll be as gentle as I can."

"James, no."

He pulled up the chiffon and caressed her thighs. He held her down as he stripped away the layers of underclothing.

"Stop it, now," Rachel shouted, as she repeatedly slapped his face, beat his back with her fists, and tried with no success to shove him off her. James used his knees to pull her legs up into position. His force of entry was strong, and she screamed in pain. His thrusts were powerful and quick, and she thought her lower body was being ripped apart.

"Oh god, oh god, more, more," he let out a low growling moan as the thrusts slowed and eventually stopped. He stayed on top of her until his heavy breaths returned to normal.

She lay on the bed and didn't move. James rolled off and got up to grab his pants.

"That was so good," he said, "you're the best, so far."

Rachel said nothing but thought of different ways to kill him before she walked back to the Pavilion. She got up, pulled on her underclothes, and adjusted the now crumpled blue chiffon dress. After smoothing and pinning her hair back in place, Rachel turned and walked to the door and waited to leave. James blew out the lamp in Cabin Number nine and followed her out of the cabin. The wind had picked up, and Rachel wanted to die.

"Are you all right, Rachel? You're so quiet," James said as he looked to the night sky. "I think it might rain."

Rachel wiped tears from her eyes. "How dare you ask me that? How can you dismiss what you did to me and think about rain? You raped me."

"Don't you dare tell me you didn't want it," James stopped and faced her.

"Do you know what this means?" she asked. "You're going to jail for statutory rape, and I'm going to bring charges against you. I'm not eighteen yet."

"You don't act like it," he said. "If you bring any charges against me, it'll be your word against mine. You're nothing but a cheap whore."

Rachel looked for a large rock or branch. In the distance, she saw a split log. "Get away from me. I'm going back alone," screamed Rachel. "You'll go back first without me."

"Don't deny you wanted it," James yelled as he walked back to the Pavilion.

Rachel waited for James to get ahead of her before retrieving the log. She heard whistling and finally saw him on the dark trail. Shaking, and careful not to make any noise, Rachel walked faster with the split log gripped firmly in both hands. When she got close enough, her grip tightened, then James suddenly turned around.

"What's this? Were you going to bash my head in with that log?" He laughed. "I heard you on the trail." James snatched the log away and grabbed Rachel's arm. "I'm not ready to die yet." He chuckled and pulled Rachel back to the Pavilion.

"Where have you been?" Ada asked.

"On the trail, Mrs. Clair," said James. "The wind picked up, and it looks like rain." He turned around and found a dance partner.

"Rachel, you're a mess. It's time we left," said Ada. "Your father is angry and waiting for us outside."

"Where's Ned?" Rachel asked as she looked around the room.

"We looked for you. Ned wanted another dance but couldn't find you," Ada began. "He went home."

Rachel felt ill. Her first dance was supposed to be one of the highlights of her life. Now her body had been ravaged, her father was angry, and the one person she truly wanted had been looking for her. What was to be an innocent walk on a special night had turned into a shameful nightmare.

James violated her trust of men and spoiled any anticipation of passion, desire, and the natural act of love she could have with a man she truly loved. How could she live her life like this? Now she would be afraid of a man touching her, loving her, wanting her.

Rachel had read in magazines and romance novels how wonderful it was to fall in love and naturally give oneself to another. But now, she was bleeding and in pain. How could she put her parents through the agony of a scandal and a rape? The church would run them out of town.

The thoughts of Ned and her future were painfully blown away like the flame in a lamp.

CHAPTER 5

THE NEWS EXPECTED

January 1908

Ned McClure's plan to repurchase Serenity Farm didn't come without a multitude of problems. Within the last three months, he had visited almost every bank in Oden County and Birmingham to apply for a loan. With no collateral, the banks wouldn't loan money to someone considered a risk. He had hit a dead end. His plan now was to find out who owned the place. Someone had bought it and foreclosed on his parents. When he found out the name of the owner, he would approach them and possibly rent the house, work the land, and prove Serenity Farm was worth saving.

Ned decided to stay at the Clair farm after the harvest. He and Noble planted the spring crops, and he performed odd jobs around the farm. James, Wiley, and Hewlitt left town the day after the fall dance. Satisfied James was out of the picture; Ned wanted to know Rachel better.

Now that Lolly was home from college, Rachel wasn't around the farm much. Lolly's father bought a new red Ford Model T Roadster for his daughter, and the two friends rode all over the county in it.

When Ned heard the rattle of the vehicle, he looked out the window of the bunkhouse and watched Rachel get out.

"I'll see you tomorrow, Lolly," he heard Rachel say.

"It's supposed to snow," Rachel said as she slowly sat down at the dining room table.

"I thought so. I could tell by the clouds and the smell in the air," Ada replied. "You look pale." She put her sewing down and gave Rachel her undivided attention.

"I don't feel good. I haven't felt right all day," Rachel said as she picked up Christobel. "I felt nauseated at Lolly's today. I think it's the way she drives that Roadster."

"You haven't been yourself for months," Ada said. "What's going on?"

Suddenly Rachel ran to the kitchen sink. "Ada, I'm sick."

"You probably caught something from Lolly's house. Justus Hanes has too many strange people coming in and out of there."

Rachel vomited three times. Ada put her to bed with a hot water bottle and a cold cloth on her forehead. Ada went back to the kitchen.

"Noble, Rachel's ill. Make sure there's no noise to wake her," Ada instructed as she heard a knock at the door. "Whoever that is, get rid of them."

"Come on in, Ned, boy," Noble said as he opened the door. "Glad to have a visitor. This winter seems to keep everybody away."

"How is everyone?" Ned asked. "I don't see Mrs. Clair or Rachel much anymore."

"Oh, everybody's fine although Rachel's ill. Probably picked up something from that Hanes household. She can't stay away from there."

Ned placed another chair in front of the fireplace. After a shot or two of whiskey, the two men relaxed.

"Mr. Clair, do you know who owns Serenity Farm now?" Ned asked. "Have you heard any details about my family's foreclosure?"

"No, I don't. That information should be filed at the courthouse in Riverton or Oden," Noble said. "The details are unknown to me, but I'll help you any way I can."

"It seems to me that the foreclosure and eviction were too sudden, and I can't figure out why," Ned began, "My father was ill, but he kept up the payments with the money he saved."

"I know that. Josiah and I have been friends for years. I talked to him a good bit before the illness took hold."

Ned gazed at the roaring fire and asked, "Who around here has a first name that starts with 'L'?"

"Well, let me see," said Noble. "There's old man Wesley. His name is Leonard, then Reverend Bradshaw's first name is Lawrence. Why do you ask?"

"Just a romantic note on a piece of paper I found at Serenity Farm," he said. "Someone whose name started with 'L' signed it."

"Hmm, maybe it started a nickname one of your parents used for the other."

"I never heard them use a nickname. It's a strange thing." Ned held his breath then let it out. "The note and the foreclosure. I feel they might be connected in some way."

"When you have some questions I can answer, let me know," said Noble.

Ned got up to leave, and Rachel walked into the parlor. "Hello, Ned. I haven't seen you in a long time."

"I guess the cold weather keeps us inside. How are you feeling?"

"Much better. Lolly drives her motor car in a way that makes me sick," she said. "Daddy, do we have any medicine to help an upset stomach?"

Ned said his goodbyes, but he still wanted to see Rachel. He missed their walks. Maybe tomorrow or the next day. He'd have to catch her before she left again with Lolly.

Rachel tried to put James out of her mind but couldn't. She would never forget the ugly way he assaulted and hurt her, then acted as if what happened was nothing. He took her purity and dignity away, then called her a whore. If word got around about that night, he would twist the story around and make it sound like the whole thing was her fault. She was beginning to feel as if the community already knew what happened. A few times when she and Lolly walked through town, the men stared and made snide comments. Other times at church activities, the deacon's wives would cut their eyes in her direction and whisper.

Rachel's illness lingered. It was almost February, and her fatigue and nausea hadn't subsided. Like clockwork, the vomiting commenced each morning and didn't stop until noon.

When Lolly stopped by to visit, Rachel grabbed her friend and took her to her bedroom. "Have you heard anything in town about me?"

"No, why?"

"Just asking. You'd tell me, wouldn't you?"

"What are you talking about? Let's get in the car and go somewhere, okay?"

"I can't. I have no energy, and I don't feel very well." Rachel fell onto her bed and sobbed.

Lolly ran to her. "What's the matter? Tell me."

Rachel hesitated. "I don't know what to do. I'm afraid to tell you." She sat up and wiped her tears.

Lolly took her hands and looked straight into her eyes. "Tell me what's wrong."

"James Cason raped me."

"Oh no, Rachel. When?" Lolly's eyes were filling with tears.

"At the harvest dance, when I went for a walk with him." Rachel began to cry again. "Remember the books we used to look at when we sneaked into your father's library?"

"You mean sex books?" Lolly asked.

"I'm pretty sure I'm pregnant." Rachel could barely catch her breath between sobs.

"We need to tell your folks. James needs to be hunted down and arrested." Lolly hugged her best friend. "He will not get away with this."

"No, we can't. You know how bad this town is about spreading gossip and creating a scandal. This would kill them." Rachel put her face in her hands and continued to cry.

"If you're pregnant, you have to tell your parents."

Ada knew what was wrong with Rachel. She knew the symptoms too well, and she had to confront her daughter.

"Rachel, how are you feeling this morning?" Ada asked as she entered Rachel's room. "It's time to get up. We need to go into town."

"I'm okay. Just tired," Rachel stretched and yawned. "Why are we going to town?"

"We need to pay a visit to Justus Hanes. Don't you think it's time?"

Rachel remained silent and began to cry. "I wanted to tell you, but I was scared."

"You should be. What in the world were you thinking?" Ada asked.

"But Ada, I mean, Mother, let me explain. It wasn't my fault."

"Mother is it? When we have a crisis, you call me Mother." Ada paced the floor. "How can you say it wasn't your fault?"

"Because it wasn't. The person forced himself—." Rachel's voice faded.

"What? Who forced himself on you?" Ada's voice began to shake as she tried to understand what her daughter was confessing.

"Please, Mother, don't ask that. He doesn't live around here."

"He was here at some point. Who is it?"

Rachel looked at the floor. "I can't say. I won't cause a scandal for you and Daddy."

"Scandal? We're already up to our necks in a scandal," Ada folded her arms and continued to pace the floor. "Get up and get yourself ready to go."

Overnight, unpredicted light snow had blanketed North Central Alabama. But even with the weather conditions, Ada was adamant about taking Rachel to Dr. Hanes. In snow like this, the dirt roads were usually cleared early by farmers and their farm equipment. By eleven o'clock, the thermometer read forty degrees, the sun was shining, and much of the snow had melted.

"Noble, I have to take Rachel into town. Will you ask Ned to harness Old General to the buckboard?"

"Sure, Ada," he said. "While you're there, take her to see Dr. Hanes. She's in her room vomiting. This illness has been going on a good month."

Ada looked at her husband and tried not to cry. The results of Rachel's visit to Dr. Hanes would kill him, and she hid the tears rolling down her face.

Rachel emerged from her room pale and lethargic. She was dressed, but Ada needed to help with her hair and boots. The previous three weeks had taken a toll on her daughter. Not being able to keep much food down caused Rachel to lose weight and energy.

Noble helped his daughter onto the wagon as Ned held Old General's reins.

"Ned, I'd like you to take the women into town. Mrs. Clair will see after Rachel. Go on now."

"Yes, sir."

Ada covered Rachel with a thick lap robe and held her close as Ned snapped the reins.

ᘐ

Ned was shocked to see how pale and drawn Rachel's appearance had become. There were dark circles under her eyes, and her lips seemed to have no color. Even her lovely brown eyes had dimmed. He wondered if Mrs. Clair was taking Rachel to town to see the doctor.

As they passed Serenity Farm, Ned could see early green buds peeking out from under the light dusting of snow. He hadn't the chance to go to the courthouse and search through the mounds of legal documents to find the present owner of the farm. When they returned to the farm, he would ask Noble to borrow Old General.

"Ned, stop at Dr. Hanes house. Rachel and I will be in there for about an hour."

"Whoa, old boy," Ned called to Old General. He jumped down from the wagon and helped Ada off. He carefully guided a weak Rachel to the wagon step and then to the ground.

"I'll take over from here," said Ada.

"Yes, ma'am. I'll be back in an hour."

Ada put her arm tightly around Rachel and walked her to the front door of the doctor's residence.

Ned was concerned about Rachel but couldn't begin to ask questions. He tied the reins to the Hanes' post then pulled his coat tight and walked a block to Old Crabtree's mercantile. Even with the remnants of the light snow, the small community was bustling. He heard laughter and loud male voices as he walked into the store.

"Ned, good to see you," said James Cason. "I liked it so much here; I had to come back."

"Why?" asked Ned as he walked to the back of the store. What does that son of a bitch want here? He wasn't looking for anything to buy and didn't want to talk. Ned never liked James but forced himself to be civil.

"Come on, sit a while," James motioned as Ned made his way back to the front of the store. "How is Rachel? She's a sweet little thing. She's one reason I came back to town."

Ned glared at James as he smirked and leaned back in his chair.

"After the fall dance, I was a satisfied man," said James.

"How nice for you," said Ned as he kept walking.

"Well, let's just say Rachel, and I went exploring, and we found what we'd both needed," said James as he rolled a cigarette and winked at the men nearby.

Ned felt his fists tighten. He caught what James insinuated. That son of a bitch was gloating to the other men about something that couldn't have happened. Rachel wasn't the type. He picked up an apple for Old General, flipped a nickel to Crabtree and left.

Ned thought about what James said while walking back to the doctor's office. *Rachel isn't the type.* He repeated those words over and over in his mind. Old General quickly took the apple Ned offered. He climbed onto the seat of the buckboard and thought about that night at the harvest dance and what James just said. He saw Rachel walk outside with James and remembered looking for her for another dance. They must have been gone for an hour, at least.

"Ned, I need your help," Ada called out as she and Rachel stood on the front porch of the stately house. Rachel seemed to be stable and walking on her own.

"I'm fine, I only need something to eat," Rachel argued. "I feel better."

"Take my arm," said Ned as he hurried beside her.

Rachel heard the words she dreaded. "You're going to have a baby, young lady." She noticed the furrowed brow and Dr.

Hanes's stern tone of voice laced with disgust. It was official, and her mother was treating her like an invalid.

"Stop, both of you! I can walk to the wagon by myself," said Rachel.

"Get on the buckboard, now!" Ada's embarrassment had turned to anger.

The ride back to the farm was again painfully silent. Noble had to be told. Soon, the entire community would be aware of her predicament.

Rachel sat on the buckboard bench between her mother and Ned. She looked over at him and received no reaction in return. His eyes remained straight ahead, and she could read intense sadness and disappointment in his face.

Old General pulled onto the long dirt drive, which led to the main house. Without Ned's guidance, the old horse stopped in front of the porch. He quickly jumped off the buckboard and helped Ada off. Her mother's eyes were filled with tears as she waited for her daughter. With care, Ned lifted Rachel off the buckboard, and their faces almost touched. With a nervous smile, he steadied her with both hands about her waist.

Rachel took one of his hands from her waist and squeezed it. "Thank you, Ned," she said as she caught up with Ada, and looked back at him. Rachel was glad to be home, although the most painful part of the situation was about to begin.

൴

Rachel had to tell her father about the pregnancy. There were already too many lame excuses made about her supposed illness.

Noble sat in his favorite parlor chair with Christobel in his lap. "What did old man Hanes have to say? Why are you crying, Ada? What is it?"

After Rachel sat down on the sofa, she closed her eyes and prepared herself. Thinking back to the night of the dance and the

Number nine cabin, she dropped her head with shame. How could I have been so stupid and naïve to even leave with James? Nerves caused her body to shake, to rock back and forth, and she didn't know what to do with her trembling hands. Rachel smoothed her hair and adjusted her blouse before she said, "I'm going to have a baby."

"What did you say?"

"I know you heard me, Daddy."

Rachel opened her eyes and looked at her father. He put Christobel on the floor and stood. His jaw clenched; his trademark expression before he lost his temper. He walked to the window and looked out.

"Come here, girl," Noble said in a stern voice. "Look out this window."

She saw Ned taking the harness off Old General and open the fence to the pasture.

"Is he the father?" he asked.

"No, Daddy. It's someone else."

"Who is the father?" Noble's voice was barely above a whisper.

"It doesn't matter. It's mine, and I'll take care of it."

Noble pounded his fist on the table. "Yes, it does matter! The bastard will take responsibility!"

Rachel jumped as her father raised his voice. "Daddy, I don't want to see him; I hate him, and I don't want to remember." She started to cry.

"Remember? Remember what? The time you lost your purity, your innocence?" Noble paced and said with gritted teeth, "You had better tell me what you don't want to remember. And I mean right now." Her father stood with his hand up to strike his daughter. He was waiting for the answer she never wanted to give.

Rachel looked at the floor. "James Cason is the father," she murmured, "and he forced himself on me." Ada closed her eyes then looked to the ceiling.

"Wherever that scum is, I'll find him," Noble said. "You can count on it. And when I do, I'll kill him."

"No, Daddy," Rachel jumped to her feet. "You can't risk a scandal. That's why I didn't want to tell you about James."

"Scandal or no scandal, he raped my little girl, and he will pay," Noble yelled. "Do you think I care about what people say about me?"

"It won't be you, Noble, that they'll scrutinize," Ada finally spoke. "Rachel will be their target."

"Like hell," he answered.

"Think, Noble. Is killing a man worth ruining yours and Rachel's lives?" Ada asked. "Chances are James Cason will never come around Coal Springs again."

CHAPTER 6

THE SWIM

Rachel hadn't seen or heard from Lolly in months. It was spring. Where was she? She'd sent numerous messages to Lolly, but they all came back unopened. Rachel was tired of talking to only her parents. She needed someone else to talk to; someone to confide in, and Ned was working in the barn.

The last three months were spent in hiding. Many times, she had watched Ned through the window but went to her room when he came to the house. Her body had changed dramatically, and she was tired of concealing it with oversized coats and wool shawls.

"Busy, Ned?"

"Hi, Rachel." Ned lowered his eyes as the expression confirmed his disconcertment. "No, not really."

"I've missed seeing you and taking our walks. What with the winter and all."

"Yea, I've been busy with the spring crops, but I should be outside more now that warm weather's coming," he said.

The conversation felt awkward. "It's obvious Daddy didn't tell you about my condition," she said.

"I'm sorry for the confused look on my face, but I'm not shocked," said Ned. "I suspected it when I drove you to the doctor that day."

Rachel looked down and started to cry. She didn't want Ned, of all people, to be disappointed in her.

He lifted her chin with his finger and said, "Rachel, it's going to be okay. I know you don't love him."

"So, you know," she said. "James raped me. You're the one person I can trust. That's the first time I've used that word to anyone, except Lolly, to describe that night." Rachel fell into his chest and sobbed. "Daddy wants to kill him., I want to kill him."

"You and your father aren't going to kill anybody," he began, "much less somebody like James. It wouldn't be worth anyone's time." Ned put his arms around her.

"I know the entire community is talking about me."

"This town is full of shameful people. Don't let them fool you," he said. "The ones that run the church and sit in the first pew are the worst of all." Ned took both of her hands. "Remember, you and your character are worth one hundred of them."

"Thank you for making me feel a little better," Rachel said. She perched on her tiptoes and kissed him on the cheek.

He took her face in his hands and gave her a gentle kiss on the forehead.

She smiled and said, "I won't keep you." Rachel turned to walk away then stopped. "Let's always confide in each other."

Suddenly Lolly drove up in a cloud of dust. "Rachel, James Cason is back."

"What? Where have you been? I've been trying to reach you for months," Rachel said. "Were you avoiding me?"

"Rachel, did you hear what I said?"

"Yes. Did you hear my question?" Rachel asked.

"Daddy sent me to Europe with Sally, the maid," she began. "He doesn't want us to be friends anymore. I protested and told him I didn't want to go because I knew you needed me, but he wouldn't listen. I got back today, and I saw James in town." Lolly ran over to hug her friend. "Don't worry; I'm home for good."

"I'm so glad." Rachel said. "I've missed you." She prayed James would stay away from her. She didn't want to see his face again. This baby was hers and hers alone. Dr. Hanes estimated the baby would be born in August. Maybe James would be long gone by then.

Rachel appreciated the respectful way Ned treated her. He always smiled at her, and when he had time, they sat under the large old oak tree in front of the house. As he spoke, his lips barely moved, and she tried not to love the sound of his gentle voice. She knew they had no future together.

"My father taught me how to farm when I was small. We would ride our old horse together and plow the fields," Ned said as he lay back on the soft ground. "That's why I love Serenity Farm. It's part of me."

"How it must have hurt when you had to leave," said Rachel. "I feel the same about this farm."

"The day we left, my mother and I had tied all we could onto our wagon. She was forced to leave all the furniture she inherited from her parents to pay off the outstanding debt." Ned wiped his eyes with his sleeve. "My father was so ill, and we had nowhere to go. The future was hopeless."

"Where are your parents now?"

"Gone. Both dead."

Rachel wasn't expecting that. She assumed they lived somewhere nearby and Ned left home to earn money to send them. "I'm sorry, I didn't know."

"How could you know? I don't like to talk about it, but I don't mind talking about them with you."

The spring day was warm, and after an hour, Rachel wanted to take a swim in the creek. She decided the warm natural springs in Cain Creek were just what she needed.

Ned had fallen asleep, and she woke him with a nudge. "How 'bout a swim?"

He looked a little shocked. "Are you asking me to swim with you? Isn't it forbidden for unmarried men and women to swim together?"

"So what? They're already gossiping about me. Anyway, I've been swimming there anytime I wanted to since high school," she said. Rachel got up and began to walk toward the road.

"I'll meet you there," called Ned. "I need to check on Old General and lock up the bunkhouse."

~

In less than ten minutes, Ned found the tree branch that marked the path. He followed it until he found Rachel's clothes spread out on the overgrown brush he had always used. Is she naked?

He walked to the clearing and saw her head come out of the water. "How's is it?"

"Wonderful, come on in," Rachel said.

He took off his shirt and started for the water. Before he could dive in, Rachel waved, and he stopped.

"Be natural; take your pants off," she shouted. "It's the only way to swim."

"Rachel? You sure?" He looked around. But for what? No one was around. For the first time, though, he felt embarrassed to shed his clothes.

"I'm sure." When Rachel saw Ned's perfect body again, she shivered in the warm water as chills ran up and down her spine. He walked into the water then took a shallow dive. His head came up in front of her.

"Did you know Lolly and I used to watch you swim here after school?"

"Sure, I did. I could see you two behind those bushes over there to the left," Ned said as he pointed to the exact location.

"You stinker," Rachel said as they both began to laugh. "I can't believe old Mrs. Crabtree didn't catch us. You know, since the first day I saw you swim, I was determined to teach myself how to glide like an eel through the water, like you."

"It's the only way to swim," Ned began, "slow and natural, like a bream."

"The warm springs feel so good to me now," she said. "You can't wear clothes and experience what nature offers us in these waters." Rachel turned and began to glide through the water, and Ned followed close behind. When they stopped, their bodies touched.

"Did you know the Mountain Lodge Hotel had the best season ever last year?" she asked, trying to steer her mind elsewhere. "Most of the cabins were rented for the entire summer…."

"Shh, don't talk, listen," Ned whispered. "Do you hear the male cardinal calling out to his mate?"

"Yes." Rachel listened intently. "I also hear the spring peeper frog. He's the loudest one of all."

Their eyes met. Rachel smiled and waited for Ned to lean in and kiss her. She wanted him to. She reached under the water and put her hands on his muscular chest. He responded with a soft, gentle kiss on her lips.

"Rachel, we can't," he said. "We shouldn't be here like this."

"Ned, please forgive me for being so bold, but my feelings for you began the first day I saw you working with Daddy in the orchard," she began to cry. "I know I'm tainted, and no man in their right mind would want me…."

"No, don't say that." Ned grabbed her and held her as he continued to tread water.

"Ned, we must be careful and not be seen anywhere together. The town will talk and say you're the father."

"Does anyone know it's James, besides your parents and Lolly?"

"Just you."

"Well, I can take care of myself," he said. "Let's swim back to the bank." Ned helped her out of the water, and their naked bodies glistened as the sun shone on the droplets. Ned took her hand and led her to the brush to dress.

CHAPTER 7

A SURPRISE VISIT

"Daddy, I'm home now, and I will see Rachel," Lolly stomped her foot. "She needs me."

"That tramp needs nothing but a lesson on abstinence," Dr. Hanes said. "I don't want you around her or the scandal that's brewing in town."

"It wasn't her fault," she said. "She isn't a tramp, and I'm going back over there today. You forced me to leave here in January. Now it's spring. You can't stop me."

"If you do, there will be no Roadster, no freedom, no nothing." Dr. Hanes lit his cigar and left the room.

Lolly stormed upstairs and slammed her door. I'm going anyway. He'll never know.

❧

James Cason had been in town for two months and spent most of his time at the Drops Inn or Crabtree's. There were no decent girls in Coal Springs to drink or dance with except Rachel Clair and Lolly Hanes. He had been avoiding them, but now might be a good time to visit Rachel. He'd made a woman out of her once.

It took twenty minutes to walk to the Clair farm from town. James picked a bouquet of wildflowers and strolled the long drive to the main house. Old General grazed in the pasture, and Ned banged on the plow.

"Hello, Ned. Are you working here again?" James asked.

"I never left."

"I see," he said. "Do you know if Rachel's home?"

"Not sure," Ned answered, never looking up. He continued to bang on the harness of the plow.

James went to the screened door and knocked.

"Come in, Ned," a female voice called from the kitchen.

"Hello, Rachel," he said as his eyes went directly to her swollen abdomen.

"What do you want?" Rachel asked through clenched teeth. "I think you should leave."

James gestured at her condition with a puzzled look on his face. "What gives here?"

"Nothing to do with you," she shot back in resentful umbrage.

"When did you and Ned get married?" James asked. "I always knew he wanted you for himself."

"I'm not married, and Ned had nothing to do with this," she gestured toward her growing abdomen. "Think about the harvest dance, Cabin Number nine," she shouted.

James wasn't expecting that. He hadn't seen Rachel in seven months, and he comes back to this? "Are you sure about that?" James asked. "You're lying. How do I know who you have relations with?" His affable demeanor changed in an instant.

"How can you show your face around here?" she asked, trying not to shout. "You're the only one. I've been with no one else," Rachel said with balled fists. "You ruined everything for me when you raped me." Rachel's composure was at the breaking point, and her intense glare seared through him.

"I have to go." James threw the flowers on the dining room table and stumbled out the front door.

"You'd better leave," Rachel shouted. "Don't ever come near me again."

He could still hear her voice as he leaped off the front steps.

"I'll be damned," James said under his breath. He thought his luck with all the girls so far had been pretty good, but now one was pregnant. "Damn it!"

"What's wrong with you? Didn't she want to see you?" Ned asked, accompanied by a sarcastic grin.

"It seems I'm going to be a father. Wasn't expecting that."

"You know how that happens, do you not?"

James put his hands in his pockets, turned on one heel, and hurried toward the road.

Rachel realized she shouldn't have told James the baby was his. He'd been away from Coal Springs for seven months, but all she could think about during that time was how much she loathed him and what she would do if he returned to Coal Springs. He caused unhealthy anger within her because of what he did, and she didn't know that kind of hate existed in a human being. Rachel wanted to kill him, but she wasn't capable of such an act. James's selfish and violent aggression ripped her body and damaged her spirit. She regretted not pressing charges against him, but it was his word against hers. If the truth were out about her condition and the assault, the entire community would ridicule her and the baby. It was traumatic enough to tell her father.

"I wonder why he left so soon?" Ned asked as he poked his head in the screen door.

"I told him the baby was his."

"No wonder," Ned said. "What will you do if he comes back?"

As Ned closed the door and returned to the plow, Rachel thought. *James better not come back.*

The spring day was warm, and Rachel hung the last bit of laundry on the line. Ada and Noble weren't home, Ned wasn't around, so she sat in the wicker chair under the old oak tree. She enjoyed being alone, and the breeze felt good. She lay her head back and thought of Ned and how much she loved him, but she was about to bear another man's child. She closed her eyes and woke to the sound of Old General jingling his harness.

"Let's take a ride. I want to show you something," said Ned as he pulled the horse's reins in her direction.

Rachel sat up and brushed the loose hair out of her eyes. "Where?"

"You'll see," he said with a smile. "Today, I have the time to take you there."

Where could he be taking her? She knew every private and public place in town. She stepped up on the buckboard as Ned took her hand and helped her gently into the seat. He jumped on and grabbed the reins.

"Let's move, ole boy," he called to Old General.

Ned drove the buckboard down the main road toward town. Rachel noticed how the purple wisteria overtook most of the woods on both sides of the road. She loved its sweet smell. When she looked over at Ned, he smiled and stopped in front of Serenity Farm.

"I want to show you our old farm. I'm planning to save enough money to repurchase it," Ned said while squinting into the sun. "My parents loved this farm, and I intend to keep it in the family."

"You must love it, too," Rachel said.

"I do."

"What happened to your parents?" she asked. "I hope you don't mind my asking."

A look of sadness came to his face. "No, I don't mind." He looked away and wiped his eyes. "They died within five days of each other. My father suffered from consumption and took a turn for the worse. My mother cared for him."

Rachel took out her handkerchief and wiped his eyes. "No one is safe from it."

"They call it 'the Great White Plague.' We moved to Birmingham after we left Coal Springs, and the only housing we could afford was in a seedy part of town. He couldn't work, so I took a job at Sloss Furnace." He took a deep breath. "My father lost a lot of weight and was so pale. There's no medicine for it."

"Did your mother suffer from consumption, too?" Rachel asked.

"No, I don't think so. My mother, Leona, died five days later. The doctor said it was from a broken heart." Ned composed himself and shook his head. "My parents were never the same after losing the farm."

"I didn't mean to pry," she said. "I want you to confide in me, remember?"

"I'm used to it now. The first year was the hardest," Ned said, continuing to wipe his eyes. "Let's go in and look around."

Rachel and Ned walked through the old rusty gate into the overgrown front yard. The place had been beautiful when the McClure's lived there. She remembered passing it and admiring the variety of color from the large old azaleas. Now, those azaleas were spindly and covered in weeds. A few red, pink, and purple blooms were visible through the thick invasive leaves and vines. Rachel noticed the blooming pink and white dogwood trees surrounding the house. At least those blooms escaped the stranglehold.

They climbed the rotten steps to the front door, and Rachel saw the Serenity Farm sign dangling from one hook. There wasn't a way to straighten it, so she ran her fingers over it and looked at Ned.

"Why is the farm abandoned now?" she asked. "Didn't someone buy it?"

"Yes, but I don't know who. Come on; let's go in."

They opened the unlocked front door and found evidence the vagrants had returned. Trash, empty whiskey bottles, and wadded up paper bags were scattered around the first floor. Ashes and burned wood remained in the fireplace.

"This old house is beautiful," Rachel said. "I remember when you lived here. I wish we could clean away all the brush and repair the house. I hate to see it like this."

"Let's go upstairs," he said. Ned led Rachel up the stairs and pointed out the dangerous steps. He held on to her as she gripped the loose railing.

"I love this house," she whispered, then looked up at him. "I hope you get it back."

"My parents didn't go out much, but they filled this house with laughter, warmth, and love," Ned said. "My mother was a loving soul. My father worked this farm himself until he got sick. I helped him after school since he thought education was essential to my future." He led Rachel into his parent's room.

Ned showed her the bookcase with the secret compartment. The velvet box was still there, and it remained empty.

"I wonder what was kept in there?" Rachel asked. "What a great place to hide things."

"My mother kept the few valuables she had in there."

After going back downstairs and exploring the cupboards, Rachel's hopes were dashed when they found nothing. She wanted to retrieve something of Ned's family. Something he could take with him; an item from his home. She noticed his somber mood but kept silent. There would be nothing she could say or do to make his sadness go away.

Ned reached in his pants pocket. "Look, I found this the first time I came back to the farm last fall." He showed her a yellowed piece of paper. "It was in the velvet box."

She held the paper as they walked outside. "What is it?" She unfolded it and read the note to his mother signed "L."

"Who is this person? Do you know?" She tried to mask her obvious shock.

"I don't know, but I'm determined to find out. It may take a while, but I won't stop until I find out who owns this farm and who signed this note to my mother."

CHAPTER 8

RACHEL'S BABY

Lolly knew Rachel was a victim, not a tramp. Her father was acting high and mighty, but Dr. Justus Hanes was nothing but a fake. He might be wealthy and the only doctor in town, but she knew all about his devious conduct at night. He would sneak in the house after midnight, thinking she couldn't hear him. He knocked over chairs, ran into tables, and fell up the stairs. A few times, she heard a female voice. After he called Rachel a tramp, Lolly lost all respect for her father.

Dr. Hanes, it seems, was the leader of the underhanded and manipulative members of the Church of Coal Springs. Lolly knew all about these so-called pillars of the community since she knew where her father hid the key to his private library. The sordid facts on all of them were kept in their medical files.

Even though he kept his library door locked, Lolly could use a hatpin to open it. Dr. Justus Hanes kept the key to the private files under the rug in his library and had no idea his daughter knew the location. She'd been looking at his medical files for years. Lolly knew who had syphilis, gonorrhea, and other causes of death. She also knew who the alcoholics were and most of the women who bore illegitimate babies. The names shocked her, and some sat in the first row at church on Sundays.

As she poured through the latest files, Lolly came across Rachel's. She found the line that stated the name of the father, but it was blank. "Good," she said. She continued to thumb through the files and came across Josiah McClure's. All that was recorded in the file was 'consumption.' That wasn't a secret. She closed the file, put it back in its proper place, and locked the drawer. Replacing the key, Lolly left the office and walked outside to the porch.

She sat on the front steps of the stately house and saw Ned McClure riding Old General in the direction of town. He tipped his hat and smiled when she waved. She went inside to her room, freshened up, dabbed a small amount of toilette water behind each ear, and followed him.

Lolly wanted to catch Ned before he went back to the Clair farm. She needed to talk to him about Rachel's condition. She approached Ned as he was leaving Crabtree's.

"In a hurry?" Lolly greeted with a smile, then blushed.

"No, not this time. I usually am, though." He untied Old General and placed the supplies purchased behind the saddle. As he put his foot in the stirrup, Lolly kept her eyes on him and continued to smile.

He noticed. "Can I do something for you, Lolly?"

"No," she answered while looking away.

"Okay, then, I'll see you around." Ned mounted the old horse and tipped his hat to her again. "Let's go, boy."

"Wait!" she shouted. "Would you mind walking with me back to my house? I want to talk to you about Rachel."

"I guess I can for a few minutes."

He dismounted and began to walk with her as he pulled Old General behind them.

"You know why my father sent me to Europe for two months, don' t you?" Lolly asked. "He forbids our friendship and thinks Rachel's a tramp because of her pregnancy."

"That's not true, and he knows it," Ned replied, not meaning to raise his voice.

"I know that, but he acts like he doesn't. Rachel told me everything about James and his assault. I want to help her all I can. She's like a sister to me."

"Good, I'm glad. Besides Rachel's parents, we're the only ones that know the truth."

When they approached the big house, Lolly invited Ned in for refreshments.

"I'm sorry I can't stay today. Maybe some other time," Ned said.

"Will you tell Rachel I'm coming to visit this afternoon?"

Lolly drove up to the main house in a cloud of dust and found Rachel sitting in the shade under the old oak. She brought a basket filled with baby supplies, tiny gowns, and a beautiful gown for Rachel.

"Hi, Rachel," Lolly said as she got out of the Roadster with the basket.

"I can't believe you're back. What's this?" Rachel asked. She opened the basket and almost cried. "Oh Lolly, you always know what I need."

"I wanted to come back sooner, but Daddy is keeping a strict eye on me since I returned from Europe." She said as she looked closely at Rachel. "Pregnancy agrees with you. You look beautiful."

"I'm a cow. The baby's due soon, and I'm so uncomfortable."

"I talked to Ned this afternoon. Did he tell you I was coming?"

"He told me," Rachel said. "Did he also tell you James came to see me recently and how he quickly he left when I told him the baby was his?"

"No, and you don't have to see him again," Lolly said. "Anytime you need me; I'll be here, no matter what. We're like sisters, as well as best friends."

James fled Coal Springs for Anniston Alabama after Rachel dropped the bombshell about the baby. It was now early August, and Old Crabtree had probably posted flyers listing local farms hiring field hands for the fall harvest. It was time to hitch a ride back to Coal Springs.

During the two months he was away, James had time to think. He decided to try and walk the straight and narrow. The seedy life of a drifter was all he knew, but now it had to come to an end. He was about to become a father, so Rachel said, and it would be an ideal explanation for settling down and having a permanent home. His thoughts during the previous two months were on nothing but how Rachel would inherit the Clair farm one day. He had an idea, but how to put the plan into action was going to be difficult.

"I appreciate the ride, sir," James shouted as he jumped off the ice wagon. The old gentleman had picked him up in Riverton and dropped him off in front of Crabtree's. There were flyers nailed to the wall by the entrance. The first one was old man Foley's farm. The flyer behind that one was the Abner Jonas farm. The third was Noble Clair's. James tore that paper off the nail and read more.

FARMHANDS NEEDED FOR FALL HARVEST
ALL INQUIRIES WELCOME
START DATE   AUGUST 15
NOBLE CLAIR FARM   ASK FOR DIRECTIONS

He folded the flyer and put it in his pocket so no other interested parties could inquire. This job was his, and he could begin his well-thought-out plan to own the Clair farm.

Not knowing how Rachel would react when she saw him again, James approached the dirt drive and walked toward the barn. It was early, and he heard male voices. He walked around the structure to find Noble Clair and Ned.

"Hello," James shouted. "Noticed your flyer at Crabtree's for fall harvest work."

The two men stopped and turned around. "Get off my property," said Noble. "I need no help from your kind."

James looked at Noble. "You sure, Mr. Clair?"

"Oh, I'm sure. Even if I had a spot, you wouldn't get it," Noble said as he turned his back on James.

"Is it because of Rachel, Mr. Clair? Is it because I'm the father of her baby?" James asked as he watched Ned hold a hostile Noble back from attacking James. "I've been away and made some important decisions."

"Your decisions have nothing to do with us, and that includes Rachel," said Noble.

"What if I want to marry her? I want to settle down with her and our baby," James said as he stepped closer. "I'm serious, Mr. Clair. I want to ask you for her hand in marriage."

"Noble, Ned! Come quick!" Ada shouted.

The three men turned and ran to the house. "What is it?" Noble asked, catching his breath.

"Rachel is about to have the baby. Get Dr. Hanes, NOW!"

"Ned, ride to town and get the doc. The baby's coming!"

"I will, Mr. Clair. Please let me," James said.

"No, Ned, you go. Go, boy! And hurry!"

"Let him go, Noble. I don't want James near Rachel," yelled Ada.

James ran to the doctor's house. He arrived in a little under ten minutes and knocked on the door. Sally, the maid, answered, and he ran around her to the doctor's office.

"Rachel's having the baby, now!" James said, trying to stay calm.

"Ada, it hurts!" Rachel screamed as she held tight to the bedpost. "Was it like this when you had me?" Rachel asked Ada between breaths. "The baby's coming. I can feel it!"

Ada held her daughter's hand as the labor pains increased. "Noble, hurry in here and stay with her so I can get clean bedding and towels."

"Mother, it's moving down. I have to push!" Rachel cried. "Help me, Daddy."

"Noble, we need the doctor!" Ada shouted. "The baby's not waiting!"

"Ned boy, run to the road and see if the doctor's coming," Noble shouted.

In a few minutes, Ned returned. "I didn't see him."

Rachel felt the room spinning. She felt nauseous then limp.

"Noble, Rachel has passed out! What can we do? The baby's coming now!" Ada patted Rachel's face. "Wake up. We can't do this without you."

When Ned hurried into the room, Rachel was still, and her face was pale. "Mrs. Clair, get some smelling salts. Mr. Clair, get more clean towels or sheets. We'll need all you have."

Ada came back with the smelling salts and waved them under Rachel's nose. She woke up, and the pains began again.

"I have to push!" she screamed. "I'm scared, Ned."

"Ned, you need to leave the room," Ada said with a shaky voice.

"Please let me stay, Mrs. Clair, just until the doctor gets here. I've delivered calves before." Ned took Rachel's hand and wiped the perspiration off her forehead.

"Ned, help me," Rachel screamed. "It's not waiting."

Ned pulled up Rachel's dress to check the position of the baby. "I can see the baby's head," he said. "This baby's crowning. Mrs. Clair, I need rubbing alcohol to disinfect my hands."

"Oh, my lord, oh, my lord," Ada mumbled as she found the alcohol.

After Ned poured the alcohol over his hands, Rachel screamed in pain then pushed. Ned took hold of the baby's head and gently pulled. This birth was completely different than delivering a calf. The baby's shoulders seemed to be stuck. He was forced to jerk Rachel's body from one side to the other to free them.

"Ned, stop. I can't do it anymore. The pain…" Rachel screamed, "I'm going to faint."

The last jerk freed the shoulders and completed the delivery.

"You have a beautiful little girl," Ned said.

Rachel's eyes filled with tears when Ned gave her baby a gentle slap and then heard her first cry. "I can't believe it's ov…."

"Rachel, wake up," Noble shouted and shook his daughter. "She's out again."

"I'll take over now," said Dr. Hanes as he hurried into the room. He checked the child, cut the cord, then shook Ned's hand for a job well done. He asked everyone to leave the room except Ada. "Rachel is my concern now."

Ned left the room with Noble and passed James waiting in the parlor. Noble picked up Christobel and went to his bedroom.

"How is she?" asked James.

"It's a girl, but I doubt you care," said Ned with disgust. "Why are you here, anyway?"

"Rachel was having my baby. I'm here to ask her to marry me."

"Like hell, she'll marry you," said Ned. "I know you assaulted her. She hates you."

"We'll see," said James.

Ned went to the bunkhouse and punched a hole in the wall. James Cason was not going to marry Rachel. He'd see to that.

"James, fetch Noble," said Dr. Hanes. "We have a problem."

James knocked on Noble's bedroom door and waited for a response.

"Come in," he said.

James walked into the room. "Dr. Hanes wants you in the parlor."

"You get out of this house," Noble shouted. "You have no business here."

"Mr. Clair, there's a problem. And I think it's with Rachel."

James was scared. No woman had ever made him feel scared. He was afraid something might happen to her. He followed Noble into the parlor where Dr. Hanes waited with a grim look on his face. He could see Ada sitting next to the bed holding Rachel's hand.

"I'm mighty concerned about your daughter. She's lost a lot of blood, and I'm not sure I can get her stabilized. It's going to be a while before you can see her on a regular basis."

"Oh, dear God," said Noble. "What can we do? What about the baby? Will Rachel be able to take care of her?"

"I'll call in a nurse to take care of the baby. Ada can't take care of Rachel, the baby, and you," the doctor said.

"I'll stay and take care of the baby," James said. "I think it's my responsibility."

"It may be, but Rachel wants nothing to do with you, and neither do we," Noble said. "No, it's out of the question."

"Think about it, Noble," Dr. Hanes said. "He is the father."

"Over my dead body." Noble Clair paced the floor, rubbed his chin, and smoothed his thinning hair. "You'd better be glad you're not sitting in a cell." After thinking a few minutes, he said, "Ada and I will ponder it, but I have to protect Rachel and the baby."

"I want to help, more than you know," said James. "Please."

"Daddy," Rachel called out in a weak voice. "Where's Ned? I want Ned."

Noble hurried past Dr. Hanes to his daughter's room. "I'm here. Stay quiet."

"Where's my baby?" she asked with her eyes barely open.

"She's in the cradle next to you, sound asleep," Ada said. "I'll bring her to you."

Ada lifted the small bundle and brought her to Rachel. "She's beautiful."

Rachel started to cry as she looked at her baby. She had a small amount of blonde hair and a beautiful baby's face.

"She has your coloring," Ada said. "She weighed seven pounds, three ounces, and she's perfect."

"I'm naming her Leona Josephine Clair."

"Noble and Ada exchanged glances. "You might want to change Leona," said Noble.

"Why, I like it," Rachel whispered. "Is it because it was Ned's mother's name?"

"Yes, Ned might be considered the father, and his mother's name was tarnished years ago," said Ada.

"I don't care, I love Ned," Rachel said. "And he loves me, for me."

"Please reconsider," Noble said as he left the room.

"Her name stays as it is. We'll call her Josie," whispered Rachel.

After making the difficult decision about the baby's care, Noble walked back into the parlor. "I guess we'll have to try it out, James. I'll give you one week," he said, "and you will be Mrs.

Clair's shadow for the first two days. Then in my sight at the rest of the time." Noble looked at Dr. Hanes. "Justus, this is not a good situation, but right now, I can't afford a nurse."

James stood up. "Don't worry; I won't do anything but take care of my daughter." He peeked into Rachel's bedroom and saw her holding the baby. "I see Rachel's awake. May I see the baby?"

"No. Only immediate family can go in," Dr. Hanes said, "and I'm about to curtail that."

Noble added, "You'll sleep in the bunkhouse with Ned. Not in this house. It's for your own safety. Safety from me."

"Yes, sir. Whatever you say," James said.

Being informed of Rachel's serious condition and how James was now moving into the bunkhouse, Ned felt nothing but rage. He couldn't believe Noble fell for James's bullshit. James had slithered his way back in the picture now.

After James moved into the bunkhouse, Ned avoided him at all costs. He despised James, and the less he saw of him, the better. He wanted to see Rachel, but Dr. Hanes left strict instructions. She could have no visitors at present.

Ned wondered if Noble had allowed James to speak to Rachel. James Cason was nothing but a low life drifter with nothing to offer. James left the bunkhouse before daybreak and returned around midnight. Neither spoke a word.

Knowing the week was coming to an end, Ned had to find out if James was staying. He walked to the main house and knocked on the door.

"What do you want, Ned?" James asked.

"Nothing from you. I'm here to see Rachel."

"She isn't seeing anyone."

Ned opened the door and pushed his way past James. "She'll see me." He opened the door to Rachel's room and found her asleep with the baby snuggled next to her. James stood close by as Ned shut the door.

"Rachel, I'm here," Ned whispered. "Your daughter is beautiful, like you."

"Ned, I'm so glad to see you. Please take Josie and me away from here," she said as a tear rolled down her cheek. "I think they're going to make me marry James."

"Who is?"

"I've heard them talking when they think I'm asleep," she whispered. "They want me to marry James so Josie will have a name. Reverend Bradshaw is involved as well as some of the deacon's wives. They're evil. Take me away from here."

"What do your parents say about this?" Ned asked. "Your father won't allow it."

"He's in the middle of the conversation," she said, "and he agrees with Reverend Bradshaw. They think I made up the story about the rape and believed James's denial." Rachel's voice quivered. "They say it'll help save my reputation as well as Josie's, but I don't care about that. I want to be with you."

Ned walked around the room as he tried to come up with an excuse to keep her from marrying James. The rape was the right excuse, but since the 'high and mighty' decision-makers didn't believe the truth, they chose to force Rachel into marrying the father. Suddenly, Ned had the answer.

"Rachel, will you marry me?" asked Ned. "Then I can take you away from here."

"Oh, Ned, this isn't the right way. Any other time I would say yes, but not under these circumstances," Rachel said. "Besides, you have to buy Serenity Farm. I won't ruin that for you. You'll regret marrying me, and we'd be a burden to you."

"No, Rachel, that's not…."

The door opened, and Ada walked in. "Ned, you shouldn't be here. Rachel needs to rest." She placed a lunch tray on the side table. "But I know she's glad to see you."

"I'm going now. I wanted to check on Rachel," he said as he took her hand. "I'll see you soon, I promise."

Rachel smiled with tears in her eyes. "Thank you for coming. Will you tell Lolly to come and see me?"

Ned nodded, "Sure, I will."

While shoveling manure to the clearing behind the barn, Ned noticed James walking his way. Dressed in tweed pants, open-neck white shirt, and suspenders, he walked toward him with a big smile on his face.

"Rachel and I are getting married," he said grimacing from the foul odor. "She agreed since I'm Josie's father and I already know how to care for the baby."

Ned propped his shovel on the old wagon and guarded his face against the sun. "Why? I thought you were too much of an ass to marry anyone."

"Well, I'm fond of her, and Josie is my daughter."

"Well, I doubt it'll happen." Ned grabbed the shovel and went back to work.

"Wait and see," James said as he turned to walk away. "Things work out, don't they?"

Ned glanced over at James then rested his head in his hands on the handle of the shovel, shaking. He dropped the shovel and walked to the back of the barn. He couldn't control his hurt, his anger, but mostly his disappointment in Noble. Rachel was being manipulated by her parents, the community, and the place where all people should be protected, the church.

Within the last few months, getting the name of Serenity Farm's present owner seemed low on Ned's list of priorities. Now that Rachel's future was planned for her, he had no reason to wait. He was ready to try to buy the place and get away from the Clair farm for good.

Ned borrowed Old General and rode eight miles to the Oden County courthouse. He'd visited there on a few occasions with his father when he was a student at Coal Springs School, but that seemed so long ago. The building itself wasn't extensive. It contained two courtrooms, property records, and the office of Probate. It held all the pertinent information for his research, and he was determined to find the owner of Serenity Farm in the property records.

After asking for the book of land purchases in 1905, the male clerk led him to a large table to wait. Soon, a large leather-bound book was placed on the table in front of him.

"This book should hold all records of land purchases in the county in 1905," the clerk said as he opened it to the first page. "First, find the purchase date, the address, and with any luck, all of the information will be there."

"I'm obliged to you, sir." Ned knew the purchase month was June 1905, but that was all. Assuming the search could take a while; he took off his jacket and loosened his tie. Starting on the first page of June acquisitions, Ned looked ahead to find only twenty-eight pages. All townships and communities in the county had been filed alphabetically, so he breathed a sigh of relief and began the search.

The address was Serenity Farm, 5 acres, Township 20, Range 4 East, Cherry Street, Coal Springs, Alabama. Ned knew that by heart. He slowly turned the pages, one by one, until he noticed "Serenity Farm" hand-written in a large scroll at the top of page 106. The purchase date was June 22, 1905. Ned's heart began to race. He kept reading until he found what he was searching for. Purchase price - five hundred dollars. Seller – Josiah McClure. Buyer – Dr. Justus Landry Hanes. *Old man Hanes?* Ned couldn't believe what he was reading. What did he have to do with running his parents out of town?

CHAPTER 9

THE WEDDING

September 1908

Rachel continued to gain strength with Ada's cooking and taking short walks. Even though Rachel had no appetite, Ada insisted on preparing three full meals a day. Since her health was improving, James insisted on a quick marriage.

"Let's get married now. Please. Why are you stalling?" James pleaded.

"I'm not marrying you. Quit talking to me about it," said Rachel.

"Josie needs her real father, not a grandfather," he said.

Rachel loathed him. He assaulted her once, what would he do if she married him? He had stripped away every ounce of dignity and natural desire for intimacy. Would he assume taking advantage of his wife again and again would be legal? She would never marry him.

"Rachel, James informed me of your refusal," Noble began. "I will not have an illegitimate grandchild."

"Daddy, I hate him and will not marry him," Rachel said. "He doesn't love me. He loves being a freeloader."

"If you don't marry him, you and Josie will have to go away. As much as I'd hate to see you go, you'd be an outcast around here if you don't. I will not stand by and watch the community ridicule you and your child."

"Daddy, James is a bad person, you know that," she said. "I can't believe you took James's word about the assault over mine. How can you let those so-called upstanding people from the church manipulate you and force me into marriage? Do you think James can provide for Josie and me? He does nothing. He's lazy."

"As a favor to me, marry him, give your daughter a name, then we'll go from there."

Through tears, Rachel turned to leave the room. "No, Daddy, I hate him. Don't force me." She stopped. "Are you putting those church people before Josie and me?"

Noble looked at the floor and put his hands in his pockets.

"You must, I'm sorry," Noble said. "It's all decided."

"Never, Daddy. You're only thinking about yourself, not me. Josie and I will leave this place first and never return. Ned will take me away from here."

"If Ned McClure takes you anywhere, I'll have him charged with kidnapping. You'll do as I say."

Rachel Clair's wedding day arrived without much fanfare. Since she was marrying the father of her illegitimate daughter, the ceremony would be short, with only Noble, Ada, Ned, Lolly, and Reverend Bradshaw in attendance.

She dreaded this day. James was only marrying her because of the baby. Town gossip traveled fast, and most of the community ignored them now. The regulars from the church declined her mother's standing invitation for lunch after Sunday services, so Ada stopped going to church. Rachel offered to leave town anyway, but Noble wouldn't hear of it. He called his daughter a "shining light," and he didn't want that light to go out.

Rachel heard Ada in the kitchen, preparing refreshments for the guests. She felt sick inside. Reverend Bradshaw planned to arrive at ten-thirty, and the ceremony was scheduled for eleven. Though a bit weak from Josie's birth, she'd regained her appetite and felt stronger each day. She was now able to breast-feed Josie, and caring for her was a joy. Ada tried to help, but Rachel didn't want her help.

Josie's crib was placed in Rachel's room so the baby wouldn't disturb anyone during the night. She wanted no one to touch Josie. Waking up, Josie cooed, grunted, then began to cry.

"Don't cry, little angel. Mama's here," Rachel whispered. She sat in the rocking chair, and Josie began to nurse. "Mama's marrying your sorry old daddy today. What do you think about that? I think your mama should run away, but she has no choice. She has no money; she has nothing."

After Josie was fed and dressed, Rachel found Noble, James, and Ada sitting at the dining room table.

"Rachel, I found a nice place for us to live for a while, and it's in town," James said with a grin.

"I'm not leaving," Rachel said. "You can go by yourself."

"Look, I don't want you two squabbling today. And taking my two little girls away from home is out of the question. I think we can work something out here," said Noble. "Let's get you married first; then we'll talk about it."

Ned wanted to stay away from the ceremony. He never got a chance to talk to Rachel as it seemed James watched her every move. When she tried to sit with Josie under the old oak tree, James was there. When she tried to take a walk, James was there. She couldn't get away from him. Ned despised him. James didn't love Rachel, and she was being forced into a worthless marriage. So many times, he wanted to pull her aside and beg her not to go through with it. She deserved so much more than a life spent with a low-life leech. James would soon suck the life out of Rachel, not to mention her parents. James Cason wanted Noble Clair's farm, and that was the only reason he had come back. And he was using Josie to get it.

Ned got dressed and walked to the main house for the ceremony. Before he walked in, Lolly pulled up in the Roadster.

"This is bad. What is Rachel thinking?" Lolly asked.

"She begged me to take her away. I wanted to marry her," said Ned, "but she said the circumstances weren't right. She gave in to the sons of bitches."

"Let's go in," Lolly said. "Maybe there's still time to talk her out of it."

When Ned and Lolly walked into the parlor together, Noble greeted them.

"Ned, boy," Noble said and shook his hand. "Glad you're here. Hello, Lolly."

Ned took Lolly's arm and guided her toward the corner of the room. "Knock on Rachel's door. See if she's in there."

"Hello, Ned," said James as he walked up with a stale greeting. "Nice to see you, Lolly."

Ned motioned with his eyes to Rachel's door.

"Excuse me, I want to see Rachel before the ceremony," said Lolly.

They were immediately handed a glass of wedding punch from Ada.

"I'm so glad you're both here. It'll mean everything to Rachel," she said.

Lolly took the punch and knocked on Rachel's door.

"Who is it?" Rachel asked.

"Lolly."

Instantly the door opened. "Come in, hurry," Rachel said, wearing her wedding dress. "I can't go through with this. Help me."

"That's why I'm here. You can't marry James," Lolly said. "Take the baby and sneak out the back door."

"Make sure you tell Ned. You distract Ada and Noble," Rachel said as she picked up Josie and a satchel.

Lolly left Rachel's room and joined the others. She caught Ned's attention and nodded. She glanced back at the door as Rachel slipped out with the baby. With a smile, Lolly felt she had saved her best friend from making the worst mistake of her life.

In a few moments, Rachel entered the parlor with James guiding her. The reverend took his place, and she handed the baby to Ada. Then she saw Ned and Lolly.

Rachel walked over to them and said, "James caught me as I opened the back door."

Lolly was sick inside. Did James follow her? "I can't believe it. It was free and clear when I left your room."

"I know. He was outside waiting."

~

Ned noticed tears welling up in Rachel's eyes and the sadness in her lovely face. She carried a handkerchief in her hand and dried her eyes before she turned back around. Rachel took his hand and squeezed it. Ned's heart broke.

James smiled and handed Rachel a bouquet of wildflowers. Rachel couldn't even force a smile through her tears.

The ceremony was short, and Ned didn't stay afterward. He made his excuses to Noble and Ada since he couldn't bear to watch James shower Rachel with false affection. Ned didn't see Rachel smile the entire time. He knew her heart was broken, too.

Ned walked to the bunkhouse, and tears rolled down his face. "What's the use? Why should I stay in Coal Springs, now?" he muttered.

"Ned, wait," called Lolly as she caught up with him. "Rachel begged me to help her leave. The hall and kitchen were empty. That bastard must've watched me go in her room and realized she might try to leave."

"She's doomed, Lolly, and there's nothing we can do about it. We tried."

"We can only hope he does something to cause Mr. Clair to request an annulment," Lolly said. "Maybe we can set him up to fall hard."

ꝏ

There were no applicants for the fall harvest except for the one man Noble hired before he placed the flyer at Crabtree's. Ned knew the apple orchards were producing plenty and having only two farmhands in addition to Noble could cause much of the fruit to be late for market and some of the vegetables to rot on the vine. Noble had hired four the previous year, and they still cut it close. He wondered what happened to the posted flyer.

Ned thought James would do the right thing by staying on the property and working the fields alongside his father-in-law, but his intuition about the low life was confirmed. James, being the man and acting superior, moved Rachel and Josie into a rat-infested boarding house on the outskirts of town. He didn't offer to help Noble on the farm. In fact, James didn't work at all. Ned was confused. He thought James wanted the Clair farm, but how was moving away from it going to help him get it? He wasted time sitting in Crabtree's Mercantile playing cards and drinking most of each day. Ned realized the man wasn't stable, and he feared for Rachel and Josie.

When Ned picked up the new hire at Crabtree's, he found him to be a large black man in his thirties and went only by the name of Issac. "Issac, glad to know you. I'm from the Clair farm," he said after jumping off the buckboard and shaking the man's hand. "I'm glad to have you working with us this fall."

"Yessa," said Issac. "It be my pleasure."

"Let's go then," Ned began, "it's early, and we have a lot of work to do."

Issac's harvesting skills were unsurpassed. He had worked a farm the year before in Polk County, and a letter of reference was sent to Old Crabtree to give out to interested farmers. Ned had accompanied Noble to Crabtree's, and after reading the recommendation, Issac was their first choice.

"You're the only one we hired this year," said Ned. "We usually have to turn men away, but nobody answered the flyer. That seems strange."

The two men rode back to the farm. Ned showed him the bunkhouse and gave him the work schedule. Ned wondered why Issac didn't return to the Polk County farm.

"Well, Ned, old Mr. Tidwell died this summer past. I work fo him three year in a row. Mrs. Tidwell sold the farm and wrote that letter fo me," Issac said. "He been sick a good while."

"I'm glad you're here with us. I know you'll like Mr. Clair. He runs a good farm," Ned said. "We have a lot to do this year, so I hope you and I can do the work of four men."

"We'll sho try," Issac said with a laugh.

After one day, Ned learned that Issac was a spiritual man and wise beyond his years. His broad, toothy smile lit up his jovial round face. The older man wore old worn work overalls and carried a bundle which held his minimal belongings. He prayed before the workday began and again before lights out. Noble had hired the best man for the job.

As he lay in bed that night, Ned thought about Dr. Hanes owning Serenity Farm. Of all people, Hanes. Why would he foreclose on his parents? Had they been friends at all? Dr. Hanes, being a prominent leader of the community, could've helped his father and set a good example. Hanes not only devastated his parents, but he also helped to accelerate their demise.

Ned needed to meet with Dr. Hanes as soon as possible. He wanted the facts on the foreclosure and to discuss a way to rent Serenity Farm after the harvest. He had some money saved, so he at least had something to offer the man.

The next afternoon, after harvest hours, Ned walked to the doctor's house. He claimed back pain when the nurse asked the reason for his visit. He had to make it believable. Working as a field hand could cause spinal issues. The nurse asked him to wait since Dr. Hanes had a patient in the office. After a few minutes, the door opened, and Rachel walked out, holding Josie.

Ned immediately stood up. “Rachel?” He was shocked to see her face. She had a black eye, and her bottom lip bandaged. “What happened?”

“I fell during the night and hit a table,” she said. It seemed hard for her to speak. “I have ten stitches in my lip.”

“Can I help you? Can I do anything for you?” Ned's stomach knotted. Josie was asleep in her arms. “Let me take Josie.”

“No, I’ll be fine. Dr. Hanes wants me to come back next week. He hopes to take the stitches out then. I’m so glad to see you, Ned.”

As she slowly walked out the front door, he knew Rachel didn’t fall. That bastard hit her. He clenched his fists. *I swear, I’ll kill him.*

The nurse motioned him in. “The doctor’s waiting,” she said.

“Hello, Ned,” Dr. Hanes stood up from behind his desk and shook his hand. “What seems to be the problem?”

“Honestly, I don’t have a problem. I want to discuss Serenity Farm.”

Dr. Hanes demeanor quickly changed. “Why? What does that place have to do with me?”

“I know you own it. I checked the county records.” Ned watched how the now-nervous doctor shifted papers on his desk. “Why did you foreclose on my parents and run them out of town?

“You’re very astute,” the doctor said.

“Will you answer me?”

“The mortgage was behind six months, and I knew Josiah couldn’t work. That property became an old broken-down excuse for a farm. I doubt it can grow a healthy weed anymore.”

“Maybe not, but it was my home, and I want it back,” Ned leaned forward and placed his arm on Dr. Hanes’ desk. “I want to buy it.”

“The farm isn’t for sale. The subject of Serenity Farm is closed. Good afternoon, Ned,” Dr. Hanes said.

"Why did you buy it if it's not worth anything? There's a reason my parents were forced out, and I will find out. Good afternoon.

CHAPTER 10

COMING HOME

Rachel Clair Cason was miserable. Her only happiness was Josie. James refused to work and was gone most of the time. Where he spent his time, she didn't know. They had been married for three weeks, and the boarding house they lived in was nothing but a home for transients. Most of the tenants were the men who worked on nearby farms for the fall harvest. The only females in the boarding house were Vera Smalley, the wife of the owner, and their two young daughters, Annie and Frances. They were nice enough, and the little girls loved to play with Josie.

All Rachel wanted to do was go home. Even though she still held her parents responsible for her torturous life, Ned was there. But she hadn't the strength to walk for twenty minutes since her energy level after Josie was born never completely returned. Lolly never came around for fear her father would find out. Rachel's daily life consisted of boredom and having to live in squalor. She stayed outside as much as she could. Dr. Hanes advised her to eat foods with a lot of iron, but with no money, she and Josie had to eat the unwholesome scraps the boarding house provided.

After Rachel had fed Josie, James came in drunk again and asked why she had bandages on her lip.

"Don't you remember? You struck me last night, and I hit the bedside table. My lip bled all day, and I finally had to see Dr. Hanes."

"And I guess you told him I hit you," said James.

"No, I didn't. If it happens again, I will."

"Oh, no, you won't," he shouted. At once, Josie began to cry. "Can't you shut her up?" There was a knock on the door. "Get rid of them," James slurred.

Rachel opened the door to Ben Smalley. "Your rent is overdue. Pay up or get out."

"You'll have it tomorrow, Ben," called James. "Now leave us alone,"

Rachel closed the door and said, "Don't you ever put me in that predicament again. Now the whole town will know we haven't paid the rent. I'm going to the farm tomorrow, and I won't be back," Rachel said as Josie continued to cry.

"You'll stay here, and I mean it," he said. "Shut that kid up!"

Rachel picked Josie up and sang in the baby's ear. After Josie calmed down, she placed her in the cradle. "If you can't pay the rent, where are you getting the money for liquor? I don't have any for you to take."

"I have a tab running at Crabtree's. Nothing for you to worry about," he said.

"Hmm, how will you pay for that?" Rachel mumbled under her breath.

The next thing she remembered was waking up with excruciating pain on the back of her head, and James was gone. Josie was in her cradle asleep. *How long have I been out?* She looked at her treasured watch brooch; it was eleven o'clock. She must've been unconscious for hours. She remembered placing Josie in her cradle when everything went black. Rachel managed to get up to check the baby. Josie was breathing. "Thank God."

Rachel packed a bag with both her clothes and Josie's. She would walk home tonight even though the pain in her head was excruciating and her lip was bleeding again. Never would she take another beating or live in such ramshackle surroundings. She changed Josie then lifted her out of the cradle. After wrapping the baby in a blanket, she tip-toed down the stairs. Being careful not to make any noise, she passed the dining room where men were entertaining women of the worst kind. She heard James's loud voice and saw a woman in his lap. His attention focused on the woman, and Rachel felt confident he didn't see her. She walked out the front door with her baby and never looked back.

Ned couldn't forget the sight of Rachel with her busted lip and a black eye. But what could he do? Noble should be informed, but that information had to come from Rachel herself.

He had let Rachel down. He walked out of the bunkhouse into the damp night air. As much as he wanted to, he couldn't protect her. Thoughts of murder filled his head as he pictured James striking Rachel. No woman deserved that. The night was dark, and the only light came from a small window in the main house. Feeling a chill, Ned decided to warm himself in front of the fireplace in the bunkhouse. About to go inside; he thought he heard a voice. It couldn't be. No one would be out this time of night. It was one o'clock in the morning, but he heard it again.

He quickly went in for Issac and shook him. "Wake up. I think I hear a voice outside. It's faint, but I'm sure I heard it."

"A voice? Who be up now?"

Issac got up, and they both went outside straining to hear any sound again.

"Ned," the voice cried out.

"That's Rachel," Ned whispered to Issac. "That's Mr. Clair's daughter."

"Ned, help me!"

"I'm here, I'm here, Rachel," Ned said. "Where are you? I can follow your voice."

"Here, help me."

Ned found her before she fainted with the baby in her arms. Issac caught her, and Ned took Josie. Issac picked Rachel up, and they carried them both to the main house.

"Noble, wake up," Ned shouted as he knocked on the door. "Wake up; it's Rachel!" He continued to knock until the front door opened. Ada stood in the doorway and noticed her daughter in Issac's arms.

"What's wrong?" Ada asked in a panic. "Is she alive?" She was frantic.

"Yes, ma'am, but if she don't find a bed, it be bad," Isaac said.

"Bring her in here," Ada motioned to Issac toward Rachel's bedroom. "What about Josie? Is she all right?"

"She seems to be," said Ned just as the baby began to cry.

Ned and Ada followed Isaac into Rachel's room, watching as he placed her on the bed. Ada gasped when she saw Rachel's bruised and swollen face.

"This gal been beat up bad," Isaac said in a solemn voice. "The back of her head be bleedin', too."

Noble stood in the doorway. "Ned, fetch the doc."

"No sir, I'll go. You is her people, and she need you now," Isaac said.

"Saddle up Old General, Issac," Noble said.

"No sir, we don't have the time. I be makin tracks."

Ada came back in the room with soft wet cloths and began to wipe Rachel's face. Her lip continued to bleed, and her chin was covered in dried and fresh blood.

"My baby, what's happened?" Ada asked as she folded another wet cloth and let it rest on her daughter's swollen black eye.

Ned was worried, Rachel hadn't moved since Issac placed her on the bed five minutes before. Ada pulled out the smelling salts and waved them under Rachel's nose. Rachel didn't stir. A second pass of the salts did nothing, and she remained still.

Ned continued to hold Josie. The baby began to cry, and Ada took her to the parlor.

"Do you know what happened to her?" Noble asked.

"No sir, I can only speculate." Ned looked down and then at Noble.

"Do you think Issac's right about it being a beating?"

"Yes, sir."

Noble rubbed the stubble around his mouth and said, "If Rachel confirms this, I'll have to bring the sheriff into it. James, that son-of-a-bitch."

Ned's rage consumed him. Never had he felt such hatred toward another living soul. As he pondered ways to kill Cason, Ned noticed Rachel's eyes trying to open. After a minute, her eyes opened, and she began to cry.

"I'm home, thank God. Please don't make me leave again," Rachel said between sobs. "My head hurts so much."

"Can you tell us what happened?" Ned asked.

"I fell and cut my lip when I hit the edge of the table, and my eye hit a small jewelry box," Rachel answered.

She was sticking to her story.

"What about the back of your head? It's bleeding, too," Noble said.

"I blacked out, and the back of my head must have hit the floor when I fell. Where's Josie?" she asked with panic in her voice. "Where is she?" Rachel tried to get out of bed.

"Your mother has her," Ned said. "She's safe; don't worry."

Distraught, Noble paced the floor and said under his breath, "If I find out James Cason had anything to do with this, I'll find him and string him up myself."

Ned knew Rachel hadn't heard her father. She was still again, and her eyes were closed. Her breathing had become irregular. Even he could see that. Hopefully, Issac would be back with Dr. Hanes soon.

The old table clock chimed three o'clock. Issac had left an hour and a half before to alert Dr. Hanes of the situation with Rachel.

"What's taking so long?" Ada asked. Josie was asleep in her arms. "I need to lay the baby down. It shouldn't take this long to fetch the doctor."

"Old man Hanes probably isn't home," Noble said. "You know how he drinks at night. My daughter has been beaten up, and I have to depend on that drunken doctor."

Nothing about Justus Hanes surprised Ned. After speaking with him earlier that day, he realized how selfish and mean the doctor turned out to be.

A motorcar pulled up in front of Clair's front porch. Ned hurried out to see Dr. Hanes with Issac.

"I be apologizin, Ned," Issac said. "I had to sober the man up jus ta bring him here."

"Let's see the patient," said Dr. Hanes. "I understand she's been injured."

"Yes, Doctor, I might say she's been injured. It looks like Rachel's been beaten," Ned said with barely contained fury. "Didn't that even cross your mind this afternoon when you stitched her lip?"

Dr. Hanes brushed passed him without a word and went inside. Ned looked at Issac. "Thank you. Let's go inside where it's warm," he said. "I know you're tired after all you've done tonight."

"I wants ta help that little lady," he said, following Ned inside. "She don't deserve this. I saw her befo' her face was beat up at Crabtree Sto.' The husband ain't so nice to her."

"What did you see?" Ned asked.

"She be tryin' to buy food fo' the youngun, and James took the little bit o' money she have in her bag," Issac began, "and she say nary a word. She jus look down and left the sto'. That evenin' I seen him drunk outside the Drops Inn with sorry woman trash."

Ned took a deep breath and looked up, fighting back the tears in his eyes.

Rachel woke up to Dr. Hanes lightly patting her cheek. Had she passed out again?

"There you are," he said. "I want you to keep your head still. It looks as if you have a severe concussion. Can you tell me what happened?"

"I fell. I told you that this afternoon," Rachel looked everywhere but at the doctor. "I want to sleep."

"You didn't have the open wound on the back of your head this afternoon," the doctor said.

"I guess I fainted. I woke up and decided to walk home." She didn't want to think about it. James must have hit her, but she only remembered waking up to find Josie in her crib.

Dr. Hanes turned, looked at Ada, then shook his head. He took a deep breath and ran his hand over his thinning hair. After massaging his neck a few times, the doctor dropped his arm and placed his hand in his pocket. He motioned with his head for Ada to follow him.

As they entered the parlor, she heard the doctor say, "Rachel is suffering from a severe concussion. She mustn't move her head," he began, "that means she's sustained a major brain injury."

"What can we do?" Ada asked. "How do you know for sure?"

"It's my business to know," Dr. Hanes said. "She needs rest and quiet. The brain recovers during sleep. It might take two weeks."

"She will stay here. My daughter is not leaving this property," Noble said. "We'll care for her, no one else."

"There's something else," the doctor said. "I know a beating when I see it. In my opinion, Rachel is the victim of violence from the hands of her husband."

"I should've killed him," said Noble. "Issac, do you agree with the doctor?"

"Yessa', I sho' do."

"Ned? What about you?" Noble asked.

"Yes, sir."

"Rachel and Josie will not leave this house until I deem fit," Noble said, "and with an escort. I'll see the sheriff in the morning,"

Rachel heard the discussion from her bedroom. "No, Daddy, you can't," she whispered as she struggled to get out of bed. She made it to the door and cried out, "Daddy, no."

Ada hurried to the bedroom door. "Rachel, get back in bed. You're in no condition to…."

"Daddy, don't." Rachel pushed past her mother.

Rachel found the men outside. "Daddy, please."

"Rachel, what is it?" Ned asked as he grabbed her before she almost lost consciousness.

"No sheriff," she said in a weak voice. "It's my decision."

Ned carried her back inside with Ada and Noble close behind.

"Why won't you say it?" Ned asked. "It's obvious James beats you. You need to have him put away."

"No, I fell," she said. "Don't ask me again, please."

"Rachel, you must tell us," Ada pleaded. "He has to be punished."

"No. You and Daddy forced me to marry James. You wouldn't listen to me, and now you see what my life is. All because of the community and Coal Springs Church," Rachel screamed. "All because they fill you with nonexistent guilt. My guilt," Her head began to pound. "You're the ones to be punished."

Ned turned to leave the bedroom. "Ned, thank you for all you did tonight," Rachel said before he left. "Please thank the nice black man, too." She wiped her eyes and returned to bed.

Noble left the room with Ned. Ada remained. "May I wipe your face with a warm cloth?"

"I'll do it myself. I don't need your help. Is Josie sleeping?" Rachel asked.

"Yes, the little angel is warm and content in our bed. She'll need feeding soon," she said as she blew out the lamp. "You rest and don't worry; I'll bring her in when she gets hungry."

Rachel's head was throbbing. It hurt, and she tried to keep it still. She relaxed and closed her eyes. *I'm safe.*

CHAPTER 11

A NEW BEGINNING

Spring 1909

James Cason stumbled back into his small room at the boarding house. It was three in the afternoon, and his last bottle of whiskey was empty. Old Crabtree just banned him from his mercantile, and the Drops Inn would extend no more credit. Rachel and Josie were gone and never coming back. He had tried to see Rachel on a few occasions, but Noble Clair always met him on the front porch with a double-barreled shotgun pointed straight at him.

"You stay away from here, boy," Noble would say. "You gave up your rights to my daughter."

James was determined to try one more time. He planned to walk to the Clair house and beg to see Rachel if necessary. After hitting rock bottom, he now wanted his family. He poured fresh water into the basin and lathered his face with a small piece of Lifebuoy Soap Rachel had left. He shaved his scruffy beard with a dull straight razor and smoothed his shabby clothes. James tried to tame the dark mass of unkempt hair until his frustration caused him to cut the stringy mess with the razor.

As he turned down the familiar dirt drive to the house, he heard voices outside. They seemed to be coming from the direction of the old oak tree in the front. He stopped and saw Rachel, Ned, and Josie sitting in the shade.

"Hello, Rachel," he said as he walked closer. He removed his old hat and crumpled the rim nervously with his fingers. He noticed how she froze. "I wondered if I could speak to you in private."

"No, James. Daddy told you not to come around here anymore," she said. "Besides, I'll never talk to you again without someone close-by."

"Please, I need to talk to you," James pleaded as he dropped his hat.

"Only if Ned stays," she said.

Josie began to smile at James. "She's grown so." He picked up the hat and smiled back at his daughter.

"What do you want?" Rachel asked.

James didn't like the way Ned glared at him. *I'll eliminate that son of a bitch one way or another.*

"I only want to apologize for all the pain I've caused you," he began, "I never meant to hurt you or Josie. Please let me back in your life."

"That's impossible. I'll never leave here, and this is where I'll raise Josie," she said. "You never wanted us, just the convenience of Daddy's handouts and a free place to live."

"That's not true!" James shouted. He tried to stifle his anger; then he noticed Ned stepping closer.

"It's time to leave now," said Ned. "She doesn't want to talk to you. Can't you see that?"

"This is between my wife and me. You stay out of it!" James was not holding back. He threw a right fist and hit Ned square in the jaw. Ned fell back to the ground.

"You shouldn't have done that." Ned came back with a left. Both men were bleeding and continued to fight. Ned stopped. "I don't want to fight with you, James. Just leave."

"This isn't over, Rachel," James yelled as he knocked the dirt off his hat and walked to the road. "This fight is not over." He made sure his voice could still be heard as he rounded the corner and left the property.

"Are you all right?" Rachel asked Ned.

"I'm okay. James hits hard, doesn't he?"

"Yes, he does." She just confirmed every suspicion about James. "You tricked me into saying that, didn't you?"

"The opportunity presented itself," said Ned. "How often did he beat you?"

"It's over now. I won't talk about it again," Rachel said. "He is out of my life." Josie began to fuss. "I'll take Josie in for her nap. Ada will watch her, and we can go swimming."

Ned smiled in apparent agreement.

"Let's visit Serenity Farm first. Then we can go to the creek," Rachel said. "It's so beautiful there this time of year."

The last time they went swimming together was about this time, the previous year, and Rachel was pregnant. Ned chuckled thinking at how shocked he'd been when discovering she swam in the nude, too.

Rachel tied the ribbon of her bonnet under her chin. "Ready? I can't wait to see what's blooming at your farm."

"It's not mine, yet," he said.

When they reached Serenity Farm, a FARM FOR SALE sign was posted on a tree. It hadn't been there a few days before.

"What the hell?" Ned asked.

"Now's your chance, Ned." Rachel said with excitement. "You have to inquire."

Ned's thoughts raced. What should he do first? Talk to old man Hanes today? Why hadn't the doctor contacted him first before he put up the sign?

"You should go now," Rachel said. "This farm could be yours in a matter of days."

"Ours, you mean. Let's look around first, and then I'll meet you at Cain Creek. It shouldn't take long," Ned said.

Rachel agreed, and they walked through the old squeaky gate. Ned smiled, reaching for her hand. as he led her around the overgrown garden.

"I love this place. I know I've told you that, but I can't get it out of my mind," Rachel said. "I could help you fix the house up, and Josie could help us with the garden every year." She smiled as she walked and ran her hand over the flowering azaleas.

Ned stopped while still holding her hand. She turned to look at him, and he brought his face to hers. "I want to marry you, Rachel," he said, then gently kissed her soft lips.

"I want that, too, but I don't see how. I love you, and I want to live here, but…"

"Shh, don't talk. We'll figure out something," said Ned. "Let's explore."

They walked to the back of the house and noticed the old kitchen door was ajar. "Damn those vagrants." Ned went in first to make sure no one was there. He motioned to Rachel to follow him. When they entered the kitchen, the old wood stove was warm, and a kettle still hot. Embers continued to glow in the kitchen fireplace, and an empty cast iron pot hung over the logs.

"Someone's been using this kitchen," Rachel said.

They walked into the parlor where they found an elderly man sleeping on the floor, curled up in a blanket.

"Don't bother him, Ned," Rachel whispered. "He's not hurting anything. He only needs shelter."

"Now I know who stays here. You're right, let's go," Ned said.

Before they left the property, Ned walked the dry field where his father grew and harvested abundant crops. He dug a hole with his hands and found the rich, fertile soil he knew was under the surface. "I can bring this field back to life if only given a chance."

"Meet Dr. Hanes, and I'll wait for you by the creek. I won't go in the water until you get there," Rachel said.

"Maybe you should wait while I speak to Dr. Hanes. I don't want you to go alone."

"I've done it a hundred times. Don't worry."

"Wish me luck," he said as he gave her a loving embrace, then a kiss.

Ned walked the short distance to Dr. Hanes' home. There were no motorcars or horses parked in front, so he assumed the doctor had no patients. He pulled the handle of the doorbell, and in a minute, Lolly answered the door.

"Hi, Ned!" she said. "What are you doing here?"

"I'd like to speak to your father. Is he at home?"

"I think so. Come on in," Lolly said. "Wait here."

Soon Dr. Hanes walked into the large, elegant front hall. Lolly held on to her father's arm.

"May I speak to you in private, Dr. Hanes?" Ned asked.

"Of course, my boy. Let's go to my office. You stay here, Lolly," said Dr. Hanes.

Ned followed and sat down as Dr. Hanes gestured toward a chair, then closed the door.

"I noticed Serenity Farm is for sale now. I saw the sign today," Ned said. "I want to buy it."

"Yes, it's for sale, and I'm asking one thousand dollars." The doctor lit a cigar. "Do you have that kind of money?"

"Not now, but I can give you a deposit."

Dr. Hanes laughed. "A deposit isn't the full amount in cash. That's what I'm waiting for."

"What interest does Serenity Farm hold for you? I ask you again, why did you foreclose on my parents?"

The doctor became angry. "I'm interested because of the proximity to the railroad track. The Mountain Lodge Hotel and the healing waters are well-known." Dr. Hanes began to pace the floor. "I'm planning to tear the old house down and sell the acreage. I want to cash in on my investment."

"You didn't answer my second question," said Ned.

"Do you have one thousand dollars?"

"No sir, I don't. Not now," said Ned. "Anyway, you're asking too much. Most land around here is going for twenty dollars per acre."

"That's the price. When you bring me one thousand dollars in cash, I'll answer your second question."

Ned left the house reeling in disbelief and the impertinence of the man. Dr. Hanes was aware Ned wanted to buy the property, so why wasn't he informed? He shrugged and muttered, "He'll never get that kind of money for five acres."

ᘓ

Rachel was excited about Serenity Farm and how Ned had a chance to live in his beloved childhood home. She hoped to have her marriage annulled since the marriage was never consummated. As much as James tried, she couldn't stand the thought of his hands touching her body. Now her life was taking a turn for the better, and she couldn't help but imagine a promising future with Ned.

She found the familiar branch that marked the path to Cain Creek and ducked into the overgrown vines and brush. After approaching the clearing, Rachel removed her shoes and stockings, pushed them under a bush, then headed to the water's edge to wait for Ned. She heard rustling in the bushes and turned to look. No one was there, and no branches were moving. *It's only a bird.*

Rachel dangled her bare feet in the creek, and the warm water from the natural springs offered soothing relief. The snapping of a branch startled her. It was probably Ned. She heard dry leaves crunching close to the path and followed it toward the main road. The sound was getting closer, but she saw no one, not even a rabbit or squirrel.

"Ned?" Rachel called. "Are you there?" There was no answer. Uneasy, Rachel decided to wait on the road for Ned. She heard more crackling of dry leaves behind her now. Rachel walked faster, and the rustling became louder. Suddenly, she stopped and turned around.

"What are you doing here? Get away from me!" Rachel screamed before a hand covered her mouth and muffled her voice.

As she struggled to get free, a blow to her face knocked her to the ground. Bleeding, she managed to get up. "Leave me alone!" Again, a fist came from nowhere and struck her ear. She screamed and knew her eardrum had ruptured. She started to run. He caught her, and repeatedly punched her face, her neck, her back. She fought him, but he was too strong. Her injuries were such that her strength was gone, and she collapsed. He kicked her in the stomach, her head, and then – nothing.

Rachel slowly opened her eyes and found herself alone on the path. She tried to move but couldn't. She had no feeling in her legs, and the pain in her back was unbearable. Rachel knew her back, and arms were broken.

"What are you going to do? You can't move," a voice came out of the brush. "Let me help you," he said with a laugh.

"Don't touch me," Rachel gurgled. With most of her teeth broken, and her mouth filled with blood. "I'll get home by myself."

"I doubt that," he said as he grabbed her by her broken arms and dragged her to the edge of the creek.

Rachel lost consciousness. When she awoke, he was sitting by her. "Why are you doing this to me?" she said in a weak whisper. Rachel knew she would have no quality of life if she somehow survived.

"Goodbye, Mrs. Cason," he said as he used his foot and pushed her in the creek.

CHAPTER 12

AN UNNECESSARY EVIL

When Ned left Dr. Hanes, his hopes weren't high, but at least the old horse's ass hadn't refused to talk to him about Serenity Farm. All he could do was hope and pray things would go his way, for once.

On his way to Cain Creek to meet Rachel, Ned thought of nothing but how good their life could be together. With Noble's help, she would get rid of James. Ashamed of himself for thinking it, he wondered if they ever had relations after they were married. Rachel had never wanted to marry James; her parents had forced her. Knowing Rachel, she got all she didn't want from James Cason the night at the fall dance, which resulted in the pregnancy. If that was the case, she could get an annulment.

Ned found the familiar branch and turned in. The path looked as if the local boys had been roughhousing. The dirt was disrupted, leaves and branches from the low-lying brush lay on the ground. "Idiot kids." He reached the clearing and saw Rachel's shoes and stockings pushed under a bush. He looked for her, but she wasn't on the bank waiting for him. "Rachel!" He got no answer. Ned walked the other cleared paths, and she wasn't on any of them.

"Rachel, where are you?" Ned called. He walked back to the clearing. Not noticing it before, there seemed to be evidence of something dragged toward the water. As he got a closer look, he saw blood smeared into the dirt within clumps of blonde hair. Ned felt sick with panic. He raced around the bank, calling her name.

Then he saw an object next to the edge bobbing in and out of the water with the breeze.

"Oh no, God, no!" he shouted through tears and anguish. He saw the once beautiful face, almost torn apart. Most of the blood had washed away, but the swollen eyes were open and empty. "Oh, God, Rachel, who did this to you?" Ned sobbed. He waded into the water and lifted her lifeless body out and placed her on the clearing.

The injuries were numerous. He turned Rachel over, straddled her, and pressed her back gently to work the water out of her lungs. He felt the broken ribs and the severed backbone. After doing this for ten minutes, it was no use. Ned knelt beside the body of the woman he loved. He looked up to the sky and cried out, "Why? Why God?" Ned picked her up and began the long walk back to the Clair farm.

As he sobbed, his tears almost blinded him as he carried Rachel home. The long dirt drive to the main house seemed endless. He found Ada sweeping the front porch, while Noble groomed Old General under the shade of the old oak tree. At the same instant, they stopped and looked at Ned. Ada dropped her broom, and Noble held tight to Old General. They stood in shock as Ned approached them.

"Rachel's dead," Ned said, choking back sobs. "We were to meet at Cain Creek. We were only apart ten minutes."

Noble Clair let go of the old horse and dropped to his knees. He clasped his hands and rocked back and forth. After a few minutes, Noble picked himself up and struggled to walk.

"Let me have my daughter," he said as he held out his arms.

"No, sir," Ned sobbed, "I'll take her inside."

Noble stood in front of the house as Ada let out a mournful scream. She brought her hands to her face as Ned carried their daughter into the house. Ada's face was ashen as she began to lose her balance. Noble struggled with great effort to the porch and caught her before she fell. He helped her into the house and placed her in a chair.

Ned lowered Rachel on to her bed, and Christobel jumped up and lay next to her. Noble looked at Ned with tears and a question in his eyes. "What has she been through? What happened?"

Still, in shock, Ned could only say, "I found her in Cain Creek like this. We were supposed to meet…"

Noble sat down and cried, "my little girl, my little girl."

Josie woke from her nap. It was time for her feeding.

"What'll we do?" Noble looked at Ada.

Ada, shaking, stood in the doorway. "I'll have to find a wet nurse." She walked to the bed where her daughter lay and took her hand. She examined the bruises on Rachel's broken arms then reached across to Rachel's face. "It looks like she tried to defend herself. Even her nose is broken."

Ned couldn't stay and ran outside. After making it to the side of the barn, Ned lost the small amount of food he had eaten within the last few hours. Trying to pull himself together, Ned went back to the house.

"Mr. Clair, I'll take Old General and bring Sheriff Crow and Dr. Hanes back with me," said Ned as he wiped his swollen eyes. "Leave her as she is. I think the sheriff needs to see her injuries."

"Okay, son. We won't bother her," Noble said.

As Ned walked out the door, he heard Noble say through tears, "Ada, what will we do without her? Why did he kill her?"

Even though Old General was old, he could still gallop. Ned reached Dr. Hanes home first. He ran to the front door and banged on it.

"Dr. Hanes, open up!" Ned called. "Dr. Hanes!"

Lolly answered the door again. "Ned, you were just here. Did you forget something?"

"No, Rachel's been killed. Have your father come to the Clair farm. Tell him to hurry!"

"What? No! No!" Lolly cried. "Daddy! Daddy, it's Rachel!"

Ned jumped on Old General and was at the Sheriff's office in five minutes. He explained to Sheriff Crow what had happened. "We need to find out who did this. I found Rachel, then carried her from Cain Creek to Clair's farm. I left instructions with Noble not to touch her."

"You did right, son. Let's go," said the sheriff.

James Cason walked into his room at the boarding house and packed his old leather bag. There wasn't much to carry, but he was leaving nothing behind. His rent was in arrears five months, but he was able to stay because the owner's pretty wife, Vera, was attracted to him.

James liked Vera Smalley's flaming red hair and her thin, scantily worn day dresses with the plunging necklines. James met the older woman every week in a secluded place near the railroad trestle, then rode in the Smalley's carriage to a seedy roadside stop near Riverton. When her two young daughters weren't in class at Coal Springs School, they ran wild through the community.

"Where are you going?" Vera asked.

"I'm leaving. Rachel refuses to come back," said James. "I don't know where I'm heading. Birmingham, I guess. There's nothing left for me here."

"I see," Vera said. "Wait a day or two. Maybe Rachel will see fit to come back."

"I've pleaded with her. She won't," James said. "I saw her less than an hour ago at her father's farm."

James picked up his old bag and walked out the door of the room. He started down the stairs as Vera followed close behind.

"Please don't go," Vera pleaded as she tugged on his sleeve.

"I have to," he said. "Thanks for my room." James Cason left the old boarding house and started to walk across the dirt road towards Crabtree's Mercantile. There, he could hitch a ride anywhere.

"Is that all you have to say to me?" Vera shouted.

"Forget about me. I have to get outa here."

As James crossed the street, Ned and Sheriff Crow passed him in a hurry. He'd never seen Old General gallop.

"Do you know what happened?" James asked some men in front of Crabtree's.

"No, but I saw old man Hanes leave in a hurry, too," said one. "His daughter was with him."

James wondered if something was wrong at the Clair farm. He'd been there no more than an hour before. Nothing seemed out of the ordinary then, except the fight with Ned.

He changed his plans and started for the Clair farm. Not knowing what he'd find there, he had to go. It was Noble, most likely. He'd overexerted himself and had a heart attack, or there could have been an accident of some sort. Then he thought something could've happened to Rachel or Josie.

James picked up the pace and made it to the Clair farm in ten minutes. In front of the main house were Old General, the sheriff's horse, and Dr. Hanes' carriage. He walked to the porch and heard soft voices wafting out the open window. Afraid to knock on the door, he sat on the front step and waited for someone to come outside. Soon, the door opened.

"What are you doing here, James?" Lolly asked with tears in her eyes.

"What happened? I saw Ned and the sheriff coming this way in a hurry."

"You, of all people, should know," she said.

"Know what? I don't know anything," James began as he stood, "I'm only here because Rachel lives here."

"You killed her! I know all about how you beat her up all the time!"

"Killed who?" he asked with panic in his voice. "Who?" he shouted.

"Rachel. She's dead. You killed her; beat her to death!" Lolly shouted back as she sobbed.

Without thinking, James ran into the house and found Noble, Ada, Ned, and Sheriff Crow standing at the foot of Rachel's bed. Dr. Hanes was examining her injuries.

"Get out of here, boy," the doctor said as he held Rachel's right arm and examined the bruises. "You don't belong here."

"She's my wife," he said. "I belong here just as much as anybody. What happened to her?" He pushed his way to the side of the bed.

Noble faced his son-in-law. "You ought to know. You were the last one to see her alive, and I'm about to kill you." His face was red, as tears continued to flow.

"I'm coming with you, Mr. Clair," said Ned.

"Stop, Noble, Ned. Come with me," the sheriff said as he led James out. "You have anything to do with this, boy?" Sheriff Crow asked.

"No, sir," James said. "I saw Rachel about an hour ago under the oak tree out front. I pleaded with her to come back."

"Ned said as much," the sheriff said. "But I'm not letting you out of my sight."

James saw Lolly standing by her father's carriage glaring at him, but she said nothing. Hearing her words over and over in his head, James realized there would be suspicion since he beat her before. *I didn't do it.*

As he looked out at the old oak tree where he last saw Rachel, he heard the door open. Not turning around, James knew it was Ned standing there. He could feel the sting of his sharp stare and the coldness of his demeanor.

Ned said nothing. James watched him untie Old General and head for the barn. "I didn't do it," he said. Ned didn't acknowledge the statement.

Lolly passed him and went back inside. James sat on the front steps of the main house and put his head in his hands. In a matter of minutes, Sheriff Crow nudged him and said, "Come on, boy. You're coming with me."

"Why? I haven't done anything."

"I'm arresting you for the former abuse of Rachel Clair," the sheriff said.

"You have no proof of that," said Ned.

"Believe me, I do."

CHAPTER 13

DANDY

The day of Rachel's funeral was sunny and solemn. Ned knew how much she loved this time of year and decided to cut some of his mother's azaleas from Serenity Farm to place in her casket. Ned opened the old gate and clipped beautiful pink, lavender, and white blooms until he could hold no more. Thinking about Rachel caused him to retrace every step they took together on the property two days before. He went into the house and found the old vagabond awake and warming up in front of the old stove. A kettle was boiling.

"You cold?" asked Ned.

With a start, the elderly man turned around. "Yes, who's asking?"

"I'm Ned McClure. I used to live here. My parents and I left town a few years ago."

"I remember you, Ned," the old man said. "I'm sure you don't remember me, but I worked for your father fifteen years ago. My name is Daniel Day, but everyone calls me Dandy. I knew your parents well." He offered Ned a cup of tea. "I left this farm when I contracted typhoid fever, and my health hasn't been the same since."

Ned shook the old man's hand. "I'm trying to repurchase the place from Dr. Hanes." He took the cup of tea offered to him and sat down on one of the old crates scattered about the floor. "There's been a tragic death in Coal Springs, and I'm putting my plans on hold for now."

"Death? Who died, if you don't mind my asking," Dandy said.

"Rachel Clair, the daughter of Noble and Ada Clair," said Ned. "It appears to be murder." Ned's eyes filled with tears. He sniffled and wiped his nose. "Her funeral is today at the Church Cemetery."

"Ah, yes. I remember the Clairs. Good people. I'm sorry for their loss," the old man said. "It's your loss, too, I know. I heard you both here in the house the other day. She's the one who told you to let me sleep."

"Yes, you're right," said Ned.

"A lovely girl. I saw her in town on a few occasions."

Ned wiped his eyes with his handkerchief. "I can't discuss it anymore. All I can say is, she didn't deserve to die."

"I understand," Dandy said.

Ned tipped his hat to the old man and held tight to the azaleas. Rachel's funeral was in one hour, so he left the property and walked back to the house.

There were a few horses and Lolly's Roadster parked in front of the main house. Several of Noble's customers were in attendance as well as Mrs. Bradshaw, the preacher's wife. The visitation would be small since the word of Rachel's pregnancy was viciously passed along to every hateful Bible-thumping family in the community.

Ned walked into the house with the large bouquet of blooms. Ada led him through the few visitors to the casket. Seeing her lifeless body again was more than he could bear. He turned away. Ada took the azaleas and bound the stems with twine and wrapped them with a light blue satin ribbon.

"Blue was her favorite color, you know," Ada said as she buried her face in her hands. Sobbing, she joined Noble as he stood at the foot of the casket.

"Rachel loved these flowers. She saw their beauty even though they were buried underneath weeds and vines in my mother's garden," Ned said after taking the massive spray of blossoms from Ada.

As Ned placed the azaleas inside the open wooden casket, he couldn't help but look again at Rachel. Even in death, she was still so beautiful. Although there were signs of bruising and puffiness around her eyes and mouth, she looked like an angel. The blue dress Rachel wore was the one from the fall dance two years before. Her lovely blonde hair was worn down, almost covering the small pillow.

Ned took one of the pink azalea blooms and placed it between Rachel's cold hands. He bent down and kissed Rachel's cold lips. "How can I live my life without you?" he whispered as he placed his hand on her cold cheek, "we had so many plans."

Lolly walked to the casket. "I can't sleep, and I can't eat," she said as she placed her hand on Rachel's. "I'm bound and determined to prove James did this."

"So, your father couldn't get away to come to the funeral. Why doesn't that surprise me?" Noble said. "A little girl he's known her entire life."

"I waited for him, Mr. Clair." Lolly tried to contain the spiteful feelings she had for her father. "I hoped he'd come around, but he's tight with all the people that run this town. If he showed up here, his fine reputation would be ruined."

Noble stiffened. "What fine reputation? I know more about that man than…."

Ada interrupted. "Noble, this is not the time."

"If you all will exit the front door, we'll gather at the Church gravesite in fifteen minutes. That will be at precisely one o'clock," Reverend Bradshaw announced.

Ned excused himself from Lolly and backed into the corner of the room as the few in attendance filed out of the house. He heard the whinnies of horses and the rattling of Lolly's Roadster as they left the property. He was alone with Rachel. Ned walked back to the casket, and before he closed it, he murmured, "Goodbye, my angel."

When four men from the local funeral parlor made sure the casket was shut tight, they carried it out the front door and placed it onto a wagon. Noble and Ada waited for Ned. Wiping his eyes, he took the reins, and together they followed the casket on Noble's buckboard pulled by Old General, who wore a large black satin ribbon around his neck.

"Sheriff Crow, you can't hold me for something I didn't do," called James. "Rachel never pressed charges against me, so let me go."

The sheriff got up from his desk chair. He walked in the next room of the small office where two cells lined one wall.

"I have to keep you here. There's proof of assault and battery towards your wife by witnesses and her admission."

"When did she tell you this?"

"It'll all come out in the open when Judge Oswalt comes to town for the arraignment next month," the sheriff said. "Now, if you have the money for bail, then you can leave."

"Damn it! I didn't kill my wife! I know that's the reason why you're holding me," shouted James.

"We have evidence that you could've," The sheriff spit in the spittoon. "A dead body tells many tales. Come up with the bail; then you can go."

When Ned and the Clairs' returned from the cemetery after the funeral service, he went straight to the bunkhouse. He wanted no conversation, just answers. Those answers could only come from James. That low life had caused nothing but grief for Rachel ever since he arrived in Coal Springs two years before. Ned planned to pay James a visit in jail. He would find out what happened to Rachel if he had to beat it out of him.

The next day, Ned saddled Old General and noticed the lack of coordination in the old horse. Checking each hoof, they looked okay, and the shoes were secured. He remembered the horse's gait felt a bit altered when he rode to town for the sheriff two days before. Old General hadn't galloped in two years. Concerned, Ned unsaddled him and opened the gate to the pasture for the old horse to graze.

Ned walked past the front porch of the main house where Noble sat in an old rocker. The man hadn't entered the main house since leaving the cemetery the previous day. As he approached the porch, Ada came out with a tray.

"Would you care for some coffee and biscuits, Ned?" Ada asked.

"No, thank you, ma'am," Ned answered. "I have no appetite."

Ada set the tray on a table by Noble's rocker. "Have some breakfast. We all need to eat something."

"I can't." Noble put his head in his hands. "I miss her so."

Ada took a seat beside her husband, folded her hands in her lap, and began to cry. "Josie will never know her mother. She's inside now with the wet nurse."

Ned felt tears welling up in his eyes. The emptiness in his soul was unbearable. The beautiful girl he loved was lying in a grave in the church cemetery. Her life had been taken away, and for what reason? He had to find out why she'd been the target for such a brutal attack.

"Mr. Clair, I'm walking to town. Old General doesn't seem to be himself today," he said. "You may want to check him while I'm gone. Do you need anything?"

"Why are you going to town?" Noble asked. "Stay away from James Cason. Sheriff Crow is taking care of him."

"I only want to ask him a few questions. He has to know something."

"Heed my words, boy," Noble said as he pulled out his handkerchief and dabbed his tearstained cheek.

Ned walked down the dirt drive and onto the main road. Serenity Farm was on the way, and he planned to stop by and pay Dandy a short visit.

When he turned onto the property and pushed open the rusty old gate, he noticed the birds were singing louder than usual, and yellow butterflies seemed to be fluttering about on almost every bloom visible in his mother's garden. There were hundreds of them. It was one of the most beautiful sights he'd ever seen. A small smile cracked his otherwise emotionless face.

Ned walked around to the back door of the house and knocked. There was no answer. He opened the door and went in. "Dandy?" he called. The stove was cold, and Dandy's blankets were gone. "Hmm," Ned thought. The kettle was still there, so Dandy couldn't be too far.

When he came out of the back door, the birds were quiet, and only a few butterflies remained. Ned thought it strange that in just a few minutes, the birds were silent, and the butterflies were gone. He shifted his thoughts to Dandy. Maybe he would see him in town.

Ned stood in front of the sheriff's office and took a deep breath. He felt nothing but rage. Walking into the small office, Ned found Sheriff Crow talking to Abner Jonas from a nearby farm.

"Be with you in a minute, Ned," said the sheriff.

Ned took a seat next to the door and waited. He wondered why Mr. Jonas was there, even though it was none of his business. He couldn't help but overhear the conversation.

"And that SOB was screwing my wife. She thinks I don't know," Mr. Jonas said, "but I damn well do know."

"Now Abner, you know I can't do anything about that. That's your business, not mine, and besides, it's not a crime to fornicate with a consenting adult," Sheriff Crow said. "If you're having a problem with your wife, see a lawyer."

Abner Jonas got up in a huff. "Make sure he stays in jail."

Ned watched the fortyish rotund man leave the office. "He's a big man. I never noticed how heavy he was until now," he said as he sat down and faced the sheriff.

"He gained a lot of weight in the past few months," Sheriff Crow said. "It's all the cooking Myrtis does for the boarding house."

Ned pulled out his handkerchief and wiped his sweaty palms. Nervous at coming face to face with James again, he asked, "Will you let me talk to James?"

"What for? He won't talk to me. Why do you think he'll talk to you? I guess you can try, though."

Ned and the sheriff walked into the room where James lay on a dirty cot in the cell. There was nothing else in the cell but a washbasin and a bucket. James opened his eyes and sat up.

"What do you want?" James asked.

"Some answers," Ned said as Sheriff Crow left the room, but kept the door open.

"There's nothing to say. The sheriff has me in here because he thinks I killed Rachel. I didn't. You know I was at the farm right before it happened. When I left the farm, I went straight back to the boarding house, packed my gear, and was about to cross the street when I saw you and the sheriff on the way to the Clair farm. I have witnesses. I asked them what happened. I couldn't have done it."

"Why did you beat her, James? Do you have an answer for that?" Ned asked.

"Did she tell you I did?"

"She implied."

James sat on the cot and put his head in his hands. "I have nothing else to say."

With balled fists, Ned went back to the office. "I guess you heard all that," he said. "I have to say, as sorry as he is, he's right about the timeline."

"How's that?" Sheriff Crow asked as he rolled a cigarette then lit it. "He's in here for assault and battery, not the killing."

"I'm aware of that. Rachel and I walked to Serenity Farm soon after he left. You might want to question the witnesses," said Ned.

"I will when he's accused of the murder."

Ned walked across the street to Crabtree's Mercantile to buy a couple of apples for Old General and saw a few of the worthless regulars skulking about on the front steps. He noticed more sitting in old chairs inside. The aging establishment was the meeting place for every indolent male in the small community. Most of the customers were men since the women in the area chose to do their business at Moore's General Store near the Mountain Lodge Hotel.

"Hello, Ned," Crabtree said. "This business with Rachel has the entire community up in arms."

"Yes, sir," Ned replied. He could say no more than that. After paying for the apples, he tipped his hat then started for the door.

"Are they going to string James Cason up?" one man asked.

"That poor girl deserved it, I guess," said another. "After all, she was sinful."

The tinkling of a bell sounded when Ned opened the door to leave. Without acknowledging the remarks, he left the store. He wouldn't give any of those lame excuses for humanity the satisfaction of a nod. Ned's stomach was in knots. Knowing what was being said about Rachel hurt, and not being at the farm was more than he could stand. He understood why Noble stayed on the porch. Rachel filled that house, and her absence took everything wonderful out of it. Ned recalled every detail of their few times alone together, and how she loved Serenity Farm as much as he did.

So deep in thought, Ned didn't realize he'd walked as far as Serenity Farm. He opened the gate, and the yellow butterflies had returned. They seemed to congregate around the blooming azaleas. The old trees, filled with new leaves, were full of birds singing an angelic chorus, just for him. In awe of the beauty, he noticed Dandy standing at the edge of the barren field.

"Dandy, I've been looking for you," Ned called as he waved.

The old man turned around and waved back.

Ned approached him, and together, they surveyed the old field. "I was going to bring this farm back to life. That was my plan anyway," he said. "Rachel and I were going to do it together. We were going to find a way." Ned sniffled and wiped his eyes. "But my passion for the farm isn't as strong, now that Rachel's gone."

"Your passion for it will come back," Dandy said, "and I'll help you as much as I can."

"I'm glad you're here, Dandy," said Ned. "Knowing you're using the house eases my mind. I thought old vagrants and derelicts busted out the windows upstairs and broke the remaining scrap furniture for firewood."

"That's probably true," Dandy said. "I only arrived three days ago; the day you and Rachel saw me."

"Well, I'm glad you're here now," Ned said.

"I aim to stay awhile," said Dandy with a wink.

After the loss of his daughter, Noble spent days and nights anywhere but inside the main house. He couldn't bear to go in and not hear Rachel's sweet voice greet him after a long day in the fields. Ada was silent for the most part and saw only to the needs of Josie. Rachel's death caused them so much grief; they avoided each other and only spoke when necessary.

Old General was stricken with Equine Encephalitis and died one week after Rachel. Noble lost his daughter and his trusted old friend within seven days of each other. The grief and anguish resulting from both deaths took a significant toll on him, and his health seemed to be deteriorating. Ada's emotional state was worsening, and caring for Josie with tears, and depression added more heartache for a declining Noble.

CHAPTER 14

SUMMER 1909

James Cason remained in jail since the current Magistrate Judge, Colonel Foster Oswalt, was detained in Ferryville longer than expected due to illness. The arraignment was formally charging James with aggravated assault and battery and to enter his plea of guilty, not guilty, or no contest. Only the judge, Sheriff Crow, and the stenographer were present.

After Judge Oswalt took his chair behind the sheriff's desk, the office door opened, and Ned walked in. When he was seated, Sheriff Crow nodded, then and shut the door and locked it.

"This arraignment is to determine the guilt or innocence of the accused. There will be no statement from the accused. Now, sheriff, if you'll bring in the prisoner," the judge said.

With his head down, James walked into the room in handcuffs. He looked to be thinner, had unkempt longish hair, and a dark beard. He stood as the judge explained the procedure. "James Cason, you are charged with aggravated assault and battery upon the late Rachel Clair Cason, your wife. How do you plead, guilty, or not guilty?

"Guilty, sir."

"Okay, then," the judge stated. "James Cason, you've pled guilty of these serious charges, and I sentence you to three years hard labor in the Alabama State Penitentiary in Wetumpka, effective immediately." The judge pounded the gavel to close the proceedings, got up, and left the premises.

As Ned looked at James, his eyes remained fixed to the floor, and a tear dropped from his eye and landed on his shirtsleeve.

Ned felt rage toward him, but pity was beginning to outweigh the anger.

Sheriff Crow escorted James back to his cell and quickly returned. "That part's over with."

"Well, at least we have a partial win for Rachel," said Ned. "Why did he plead guilty? He always denied the charges."

"I think it was his conscience," the sheriff said. "After being in here almost a month, he started talking and told me his decision to plead guilty."

"Three years isn't enough, but it's something." Ned opened the door to leave the office. "Today, we have closure on the assault charges. Tomorrow we begin the painful task of solving her murder."

~

Serenity Farm remained unsold. Ned heard from folks in town that Dr. Hanes was continuing to hold out for an all-cash deal. He had been ready to give the old doctor a deposit on the farm. But now, Rachel's death had caused his desire for the farm to wane, and it didn't seem so important anymore.

Ned left the sheriff's office alone. He didn't feel like talking to anyone about the outcome of the arraignment. He would stop at Serenity Farm on his way back to the Clairs'.

"Ned, old boy," Dr. Hanes called as he saw Ned leaving the sheriff's office. "Let's go to my office and have a drink."

"I'm not in the mood."

"No, no. I want to discuss Serenity Farm," the doctor said while holding tight to his fashionable walking cane. "Let's walk."

"We don't have anything to discuss, Dr. Hanes," Ned said. "You let me know in no uncertain terms that you won't sell it to me." He turned to walk away.

"You loved Rachel, didn't you?"

"Yes, sir, I did. She loved the place as much as I do, but my feelings about the farm have changed," Ned said. "If it's any of your damn business." *What does he want from me?*

"Let's go to the house and talk," Dr. Hanes said as he placed his arm around Ned and guided him across the street.

After entering the front door of the stately house, Ned followed Dr. Hanes down a long hall. The doctor stopped in front of a massive ornate cabinet. The glass doors to the old piece encased several shelves holding an organized multitude of medical reference books and journals. From a drawer, Dr. Hanes selected a large key from a metal ring.

"This is my private library," he said while unlocking the door. "My medical records are kept in here as well as my private papers. Come on in and sit down."

"I don't have to know all that, Dr. Hanes," said Ned.

"I have my reasons for bringing you in here."

Ned sat down on a red velvet Victorian settee. He looked around the room and noticed the tasteful mahogany furnishings as well as heavy bookcases crammed with more books. The portrait of a beautiful woman hung over the fireplace, and Lolly's likeness hung over a heavy ornate credenza. A framed photograph of Lolly rested in an easel on the doctor's massive desk.

"Lolly's portrait is well done. The painter captured her personality," said Ned. "May I ask who the woman is over the fireplace?"

"That woman is my wife, Martha, and Lolly's mother," he began, "she left us soon after my daughter was born."

"Is she buried here?" Ned asked.

"No, she isn't dead as far as I know," Dr. Hanes began, "she up and left us more than eighteen years ago."

"I'm sorry to hear this, Dr. Hanes." Ned noticed a well-stocked liquor cabinet behind the large desk.

"It was a long time ago, and Lolly seems no worse for the wear. Let's get down to business." The doctor poured two stiff bourbons. He handed one to Ned and lit a cigar.

"Ned boy, if you're still interested in Serenity Farm, I might let it go for a fraction of what I'm asking. What would you be willing to pay?"

Ned was shocked into silence. "I'm not sure, Dr. Hanes. My plans are changing since Rachel can't share the place with me." Ned stood and rubbed the back of his neck. "I need to think about this."

"Of course. It's an important decision and one you can't take lightly. Just remember, I'm willing to deal with you only. This conversation is confidential, you understand. "

"Yes, sir." Ned turned to leave then stopped. "Please give Lolly my regards. I haven't seen her around lately."

"She's been out of town. After Rachel's funeral, Lolly was going on about finding out why James killed her and talking nonsense. I sent her abroad again. It was the best medicine for her."

Ned left not knowing if he wanted a future in Coal Springs or to make his life elsewhere. Two short months before, he had Rachel. His life then was full of anticipation and happiness. Without her, he felt empty inside, and his future was uncertain.

Almost dusk, Ned approached the old gate at Serenity Farm for the first time in two months. It didn't creak. That gate always creaked. His father oiled it, changed the hinges, and took it off then put it back on, but Josiah never found a way to fix it. Ned had avoided the old farm since Rachel's death but was now ready to walk the fields and look at the house again.

"Dandy? Are you here?" Ned called. There was no answer, and he called out again. He suddenly noticed the trees were full of yellow finches, bluebirds, cardinals, and more he couldn't identify. Being so deep in thought about the gate, he'd almost ignored the songbird's heavenly chorus. He noticed his mother's hydrangeas about to burst into the colors of blue, pink, and white blooms. The thick stems of her deep red Seven Sisters roses clung tight to the old wooden fence. Ned's mother's flowers had never produced with so much vigor and vivid color.

Gossamer-winged butterflies continued to congregate while small green sprouts began to emerge from the fallow fields. Ned stood in amazement as he turned to open the back door of the house.

"Ned, glad to see you. Missed you around here," said Dandy standing on the top step.

"I called out for you, but got no answer," Ned said. "These flowers are more beautiful than I can remember. Have you been tending the garden?"

"I have, but they only wanted to be free from the weeds and vines. I took care of cutting that away," Dandy said. "Come in; I have the kettle on."

Ned followed the old gentleman in and sat on a crate. "I've been offered a deal to buy the place from Dr. Hanes. Without Rachel, I'm not sure if I want to stay in Coal Springs," Ned began, "but seeing it today and knowing the land is still fertile…." He took his cup of tea and looked out the window to the lush verdant garden.

"Don't lose this farm, Ned," Dandy said. "You're needed here, and I'll help you all I can."

A noise came from the upstairs bedroom. "What's that?" Ned asked.

"Probably a flying squirrel. Those varmints like to nest in empty, dark places."

"Excuse me, Dandy. If I'm going to buy this place, I need to know about all its inhabitants."

Ned walked through the ramshackle parlor, where he saw Dandy's blanket and a make-shift table. He carefully climbed the rotted stairs and walked into his parent's room. Astonished, he faced a sparkling clean room with a bed, dresser, chifforobe, and washbasin. The window was open, and a cool breeze blew in. As dusk became darkness, Ned noticed the shelves of the cabinet with the secret compartment. It now had photographs of his parents and ones of himself as a baby. He never knew his parents to have any pictures.

Ned fumbled for a match and lit a kerosene lamp on a table next to the bed. The air was colder than usual for a June evening, so he buttoned his tweed jacket. The dresser had numerous drawers, and a large mirror hung above it. Expecting to find a family of flying squirrels in a drawer, he opened one and found a light pink chiffon shawl. He never saw his mother wear one like this. With the lamp in his hand, he looked in the mirror. There was a figure behind him. He couldn't make it out and began to shiver.

Startled, Ned softly asked. "Who are you?"

"Ned… buy the farm…." The figure spoke in a haunting low whisper.

The macabre spirit disappeared, and Ned blew out the lamp. He hurried downstairs, almost falling as he ran into the kitchen.

"Dandy! There was something in the mirror up there!" Ned was out of breath. "Who was it?"

"I've seen her before. She's a good spirit. Not sure who it is, but she's friendly," Dandy said.

CHAPTER 15

THE APPARITION

Ned lay on his bed in the bunkhouse, thinking about what he'd witnessed. Dandy implied the spirit was female, but the soft voice didn't sound like anyone he'd ever known. The image wasn't clear, just shadowy and evanescent. After witnessing the ghostly presence, he couldn't think of leaving Coal Springs now. Why had she told him to buy the farm?

He couldn't sleep from thinking about the eerie spirit and Dr. Hanes's offer. Sitting in an old rickety chair at the farm table with a lead pencil and an old scrap piece of paper, Ned worked out numerous calculations for purchasing the farm, and how each deal would benefit him. He also estimated when his crops would give him a return on his money. He wanted to be the sole owner of the property as soon as possible. Confident about his last calculation, Ned planned to stop by Serenity Farm on his way to present his offer to Dr. Hanes.

Dandy was working in the field when Ned walked through the gate.

"Morning, Ned," the old man said. "Back so soon?"

"Yes, sir. I plan to present my offer to Dr. Hanes today," Ned answered. "First, I want to evaluate the main structure of the house and decide what repairs are needed. Then I'll subtract the probable costs of time and materials from the offer."

Dandy smiled and returned to his work.

"What are you growing there?" Ned asked.

"I planted a few collard greens to see if the soil had enough nutrients to grow a mess or two," said Dandy. "With a good deal of work and tender loving care, I think you'll soon have a productive farm." He smiled and nodded his head.

Ned grinned as Dandy returned to hoeing weeds from several of the collard sprouts. When he opened the back door of the house, the aroma of bacon and eggs filled the kitchen. He noticed one place setting on the old makeshift table. A hot coffee pot rested on the old stove, and one cup sat on the wooden counter.

"Are you about to have breakfast, Dandy?" Ned called from the back door.

"Nope, that's for you. I hoped you'd be around this morning."

Smiling, Ned stepped back into the kitchen and took the plate from the table. He filled it with crisp bacon, two warm fried eggs, and poured a cup of coffee. Before his first bite, he heard the faint sound of footsteps on the second floor. Ned got up and walked to the parlor. It seemed as if someone was walking in the hallway near his parent's room. The soft footsteps stopped, but he didn't move. After a few minutes, he shrugged and returned to his breakfast.

Ned cleaned up his dishes, then looked for Dandy. He walked around the house and found the old man in the remnants of his mother's old herb garden.

"Mother used to love this little garden. My father let her grow anything she wanted here."

"Josiah was a good man, and he loved Leona. They needed no one except each other. When you were born, I'd never seen such happy people," Dandy said.

"My parents never ventured out much," Ned replied. "Listen, thanks for breakfast. I'm heading to Dr. Hanes' office after I inspect the upstairs and walk the grounds. I'll let you know if he accepts my offer."

Ned walked through the front door and inspected the old pine floors, thresholds, doors, windows, and the ceiling in each room. The gas chandelier in the dining room needed replacing as well as the hand railing of the staircase.

As he climbed the rotted stairs to the second floor, Ned recalled how he guided Rachel and showed her the steps to avoid. Sadness overcame him as he stopped and let the tears flow. *If I hadn't let her go alone to Cain Creek, Rachel would still be alive; if I hadn't thought so much about my selfish plans to buy the farm; If…if…if.* The tears of guilt and regret consumed him as he sat on the top step and temporarily forgot about the earlier sound of footsteps in the hallway.

Ned wiped his eyes and remained on the step. He looked around at the hall and rooms he knew so well. His gaze stopped at the built-in cabinet in his parent's room. The door of the secret compartment was ajar, and the velvet box lay inside. Ned walked to the niche, took it out, opened the box, and found a small note. The elegant script read:

To you, my dearest, I send my love.

We are separated now,

but I shall be in your presence soon. Please wait for me.

Ned looked up from the paper. This one wasn't signed, and he noticed the difference in handwriting. It couldn't be "L" again. The previous letter had been written on yellowed white stock. This one was on high-quality ivory parchment, and no doubt written recently. Ned placed the note back in the box and left the door ajar. Maybe it belonged to Dandy. If so, the letter wasn't any business of his.

He walked into his old room and inspected the two busted out windows. Each window grill seemed to be sturdy and undamaged while the holes in the walls could easily be repaired.

The scratches and gaps in the old pine floor planks needed nothing but a little wood patching.

He checked floor joists, roof, crawl space, water pump, then the exterior clapboard and window frames. The termite damage around the kitchen chimney and the front porch was extensive, but Ned felt confident the basic structure of the house was safe, although the building needed significant cosmetic repairs.

The farm was in good shape, thanks to Dandy. The care he showed for the garden and the healthy new growth in a portion of the barren field prompted Ned to think about offering the old man a place to live permanently. He felt good about his offer to Dr. Hanes.

Ned tipped his hat as he opened the rusty gate, "I'll be back soon, Dandy." On his way to present his offer to Dr. Hanes, he saw Lolly approaching in her automobile.

"Hello, Ned," Lolly said as she stopped the car. The loud rattling of the motor caused her voice to be almost inaudible. "It's been a while."

"Yes, it has. I hear you've been abroad." He felt the hot exhaust from the automobile. "I'm on my way to speak to your father," said Ned. "Is he home?"

"He is. What are you seeing him about?" Lolly asked.

"A business matter," Ned yelled over the motor.

Lolly put the car in gear, smiled, and waved goodbye. "Hope to see you soon." She left him in a dust cloud from the dry dirt road.

The summer day was warm, but Ned felt nothing but hope. Horses pulling wagons and a few motorcars passed him with more dust, but he was deep in thought.

Dr. Hanes stood on the front porch with a cigar and acknowledged Ned as he turned onto the sidewalk. "Good to see you, boy." He pulled out his handkerchief and wiped the sweat from the back of his neck. "What can I do for you today?"

"I'm here to present my offer for Serenity Farm," Ned said as he climbed the porch steps.

"I see," the doctor said. "I hate to inform you, but I got a cash offer this morning. The buyer offered the full amount, and I accepted."

Ned wasn't sure if he heard the doctor correctly. "What did you say?" Ned's gut wrenched.

The doctor repeated the words as Ned looked away and put his hands in his pockets. "I can't believe what you're saying, Dr. Hanes," he turned his head and looked into the doctor's eyes. "You gave me until today to make an offer. I didn't approach you with this; you came to me."

"I know it, and I'm sorry. This offer came out of nowhere, and we're to sign the papers next week."

"If they offered you the asking price, then I'll increase it with a portion of the profits from the harvests," said Ned.

"How do you know any crops will grow now in that dried up soil? Your father gave the bank the same promise, and it didn't work for him. Why do you think it'll come through for you?"

"I know, that's all," Ned said. "My father was sick. That's why he couldn't work his fields." He wasn't about to tell him how Dandy had been tending the fields and his mother's garden. "Have you walked the property lately?"

"No, but in passing, it looks rather futile to try and bring the old place back to life," Dr. Hanes said. "The house has been vacant three years and will have to be torn down, you know."

"I don't agree. What are the new owner's plans?" Ned asked.

"I'm not sure. The buyers are developers out of Birmingham and getting in on a portion of Mountain Lodge Hotel's popularity," said Dr. Hanes. "I'll find out next week."

Ned turned to leave, then stopped. "Is this your final decision?"

"Yes, son, it is."

After he'd spent all night calculating different offers on paper for Dr. Hanes, Ned felt as if he finally had the upper hand since the man sounded almost desperate for the sale. His wide range plans for the repairs on the house, sowing the seed and harvesting the rewards gave him a different kind of excitement. Ned's confidence had been high, and he felt Dr. Hanes would accept the offer. But his future at Serenity Farm had just been yanked out from under him, and the dream of spending his life there faded like the apparition in the mirror.

Dr. Hanes' cruel smirk spoke volumes as he continued to smoke his cigar on the front porch of his home. Ned turned to look at the man once more and felt intense hatred. It was evident the old doctor had the desire to humiliate him. Ned thought it gave the bastard a feeling of satisfaction. But why?

"You knew about the cash offer yesterday, didn't you?" Ned shouted. "Congratulations on another humiliation." He was hurt, angry, and most of all, disappointed. *If I ever face that son-of-a-bitch again….*

On the way back to Noble Clair's farm, Ned stopped to let Dandy know the outcome of the offer. He walked through the gate and found Dandy standing over the collard patch.

"We're going to have a good crop this year," he said. "Take a look at the sprouts. They've grown an inch since yesterday!"

"I have bad news," Ned began, "Old man Hanes got a previous offer. They're paying his asking price in cash. He signs the papers next week."

Dandy leaned on his rake and looked in the bright sun. "This is your farm. He will never take it away from you, no matter what kind of tripe he throws at you." The old man took off his weathered straw hat and smoothed his graying hair. After he replaced his hat, Dandy dug deep in his pants pocket. "Come back tonight and bring this."

Ned took a beautiful watch lapel brooch from the old man. "What's this?" he asked.

"This is your peace and tranquility. This brooch is a symbol of Serenity Farm, and I'm giving it to you now since your offer wasn't accepted."

"What am I supposed to do with it?"

"Keep it in your pocket always. You'll know what to do when the time comes." Dandy excused himself and headed for the back door. "Remember, come back tonight."

On his way back to the Clair farm, Ned kept repeating Dandy's words over and over. *Come back tonight. This is your peace and tranquility.* What did he mean? He planned to find out, but now, he had to do a few chores for Noble before dark.

Before returning to Serenity Farm, Ned took the watch brooch out of his pocket and took a good look at it. The piece was small and delicate. Its lovely design included a crystal enclosed watch face, hanging upside down by golden chains. The face was attached to a solid gold ribbon. There was an inscription on the back: *To my special one. With much love. Christmas, 1890.* Where did it come from? Who did it belong to? Could it be his mother's? Had Dandy found it in the house? Ned wrapped the pin in his handkerchief and put it back in his pocket.

Dusk gave way to darkness when Ned opened the old rusty gate. He saw no evidence of Dandy. There were no lamps casting light from any of the windows, and the only guidance he had was from the full moon. The slight breeze caused the trees to emit an eerie shadow over the fields. It was the first time his former home gave him an uneasy feeling. He loved this place, but it seemed different tonight.

"Dandy?" Ned called as he went inside but got no answer. He found a lantern in the kitchen and lit it with the matches by the cold fireplace. There were no embers. The kettle felt cold, and nothing seemed the same since his inspection earlier. The dishes he washed from breakfast weren't in the cupboard, and there was no coffee pot. The crates and makeshift table remained untouched while his own footsteps on the dust-covered floor were the only ones visible. With the lantern light to guide him, Ned walked through the parlor hoping to find Dandy asleep on the floor. He wasn't there, and the room showed no recent evidence that anyone besides himself had been in the house at all.

Ned walked through the dining room and back to the kitchen. He went to the staircase, thinking Dandy could be sleeping upstairs. Climbing the old steps, he found the second-floor hallway dark. With the light of the moon, he looked in his parent's old bedroom and found it empty of furnishings and no one there. His former room was a few feet away so he waved the lantern back and forth and cleared his throat so he wouldn't frighten the old man if he were in there. It was vacant, and nothing seemed out of the ordinary. Wandering back to his parent's room, he checked the secret compartment. The velvet box with the note was gone. It must have been Dandy's.

At once, he remembered why he was there. At that moment, Ned felt an icy sensation, and the room became cold. He put his hands in his pockets and clutched the handkerchief that enclosed the watch brooch. Out of the corner of his eye, a white light flashed in the large mirror over the dresser, then disappeared. What the hell? Was it another lamp? "Hello? Anybody there?"

Ned seemed to be drawn to the mirror. Something was pulling him toward it. As he stood before it, the white light reappeared behind him. The form was long and obscure, and a sweet fragrance accompanied it; one he had experienced before. As he waited for a more transparent image, he felt peaceful, not frightened. The unclear figure began to take shape as a pair of eyes, a nose, and mouth formed out of what looked like vapor. The long hair had a slight wave and fell about the shoulders, and the long white flowing gown blew in a breeze that came from nowhere.

"Ned," the image said.

He recognized the voice. "Rachel," Ned murmured. The image of Rachel Clair was in the mirror wearing a wreath of white lilacs in her hair. The beautiful vision took his breath. Rachel held stems of white, pink, and lavender azaleas; like the ones, he placed in her casket.

"Strive for the farm," Rachel's image said.

"Rachel, where are you? Am I able to touch you?" Ned was in awe of the beauty before him.

"Not now, but you will at the appropriate time."

"I miss you so much. Who took you away from me? I have to know."

"You must prove it wasn't James. Then, in time, all questions will be answered. I left a note for you in the velvet box. Why didn't you take it?"

"It was from you? I thought it was Dandy's. Remember the sleeping old man we saw here wrapped in a blanket?" Ned asked. "He's a fine old man. He has the magic touch when it comes to the garden and the dry fields."

"Always have the watch brooch in your possession. If it is with you, I will visit you."

"Is it yours?"

"It was Ada's. She gave it to me on my sixteenth birthday."

"How is it that Dandy was the one to give it to me?"

"I must go. Remember to keep the brooch with you." The image faded away.

"Rachel! Don't go, please." Ned stood before the mirror in a state of disbelief. He couldn't move and watched as her translucent form disappeared as well as the fragrance of lilacs. The girl he loved and lost had returned. Would Rachel Clair become part of his life again?

PART TWO

LOLLY

CHAPTER 16

LOLLY'S OBSESSION

August 1909

"I like Ned, and I want to know him better!" Lolly Hanes argued with her father. "It's not fair. You're not a reasonable man."

"I will not allow you to take up with him," Dr. Hanes answered. "Go, I have a patient waiting."

"I won't go until you tell me why you don't like him." Lolly folded her arms and sat on the red velvet settee in her father's private library. "What makes you so much better than Ned?"

"I'm going to my office. I have a patient," he said. "Come on; you have no business in here."

Lolly didn't care what her father said. She had always wanted Ned McClure, and nothing would change her mind. There were no acceptable men in Coal Springs except Ned, and she wanted him one way or another.

After returning to Coal Springs from Howard two years before, Lolly spent most of her time with Rachel. But soon after Dr. Hanes diagnosed the pregnancy, he refused to let Lolly associate with her best friend unless she was there for a medical visit. The doctor told his daughter that Rachel had turned into a trollop, was pregnant, and was considered white trash by the entire community.

Devastated and in denial, Lolly's disdain for her father was turning to hate. She knew he was nothing but a lying hypocrite, and the community had received Rachel's pregnancy gossip from him. That alone violated the patient/doctor relationship and the medical code of ethics. Lolly knew Dr. Justus Hanes had no ethics, whatsoever.

With her best friend gone, and her father adamant about Ned, Lolly spent her days alone and bored. She missed Rachel so. Her father spoke badly about Rachel, but he didn't know the truth about James and the rape. She wished she hadn't promised Rachel not to tell anyone about that. Rachel was a sweet soul, even when it came to trash like James Cason.

The way her father felt would never change her feelings for Ned. She'd loved him since high school, and no matter what, she wasn't going to let her father take him away from her, especially under false pretenses, like he had Rachel.

However, there was a problem. Dr. Justus Hanes was a powerful man in the county, and he could make Ned's life hell if he suspected any dalliance between them. Frustrated and angry, Lolly was tired of being bored and planned to visit the Clair farm and talk to Ned. She was no longer a child, and her father couldn't keep her from having a life outside of the stately house on the main road that was known as Cherry Street.

Lolly sat at her carved vanity table and looked at herself in the large mirror. She smiled at her reflection as she dabbed the powder puff to her face and shoulders. She applied a lavender tint to her eyelids, then a minimal amount of lip rouge. Lolly put her long dark brown hair up in a loose pompadour, then secured her large driving hat with the thin protective veil in place with a long hatpin. She selected her favorite day dress and matching pumps. Happy with her appearance, she hoped to catch Ned's attention.

The top speed for the 1909 Ford Model T Roadster was forty-five mph. Most of the time, Lolly barreled down Cherry Street with the top folded back at a mere forty. She left horses, wagons, other automobiles, and pedestrians in her dust and never looked back.

As Lolly sped through the outskirts of town, she noticed a figure in the distance. When she realized it was Ned, she came to a screeching stop while dust and debris from the road covered the

Roadster. Lolly turned off the engine, removed her goggles, and smiled.

"Where are you headed?"

"Back to the Clair farm," he answered.

"Hop in. I'll give you a lift. We'll go the scenic route." Lolly's stomach fluttered as Ned nodded and tipped his tweed cap.

She asked Ned to start the engine with the hand-crank. After two tries, the engine started, and Ned jumped in. She handed him a pair of goggles and struggled to get the vehicle in gear.

"Are the foot pedals in the right position?" he asked.

"Yes, I think so. I'll try again." That time the left and right pedals were in the correct position and the car went into gear with ease. After a few bumpy tries, Lolly slowly pressed the right pedal and the car thrust forward. She adjusted her hat and goggles with a laugh, securing her hands on the steering wheel. "Sometimes, I have trouble getting this machine going. How much time do you have?"

"I'm not in a hurry. I have an hour or two."

"Good. I have something to show you," Lolly said. "I hope it'll be new to you."

At last, Lolly Hanes had Ned McClure to herself. From the days watching him swim naked in Cain Creek, her secret thoughts had only been of him. She always knew Ned was different. He was considerate, kind, and had a physique like a Roman god. The only problem was, he loved Rachel and never gave her a second thought. But with all the hurt and grief they'd both been through during the last few months, it was essential to keep in touch. Rachel was their connection. His love for Rachel was confirmed by wanting to marry her and the grief he expressed after her death. She finally decided that any relationship she might have with Ned in the future had to evolve naturally.

Lolly took the scenic route to the Mountain Lodge Hotel. When they arrived, she stopped the car, took off the goggles, and untied the thin veil of the hat. Her hair was tousled, but the chignon remained tight. She noticed Ned looking at her with approval. She felt her cheeks blush.

"You've changed since I saw you last," Ned said.

"In what way?"

"I don't know; maybe you're a little more grounded. I always found you to be so flighty."

"Time and circumstances change people," she said. "My life changed when Rachel died. I'm having a hard time dealing with that and other things."

"I understand. I feel the same. Going abroad seems to have changed you, too." Ned hopped out of the car and ran around to open the door for her.

"Maybe it did. I learned a lot both times I was abroad, but I'm home now and have no plans to leave again," she said. "No matter what my father says."

The busy resort season was in full swing, and motorcar parking was abundant since most patrons traveled by train. It was late afternoon; the grounds were sprinkled with vacationers on the tennis courts and swimming pool. The Pavilion, situated over the sulfur springs, was the starting point for guests and local groups to begin a climb up Black Top Mountain.

"Come on. Let's climb the mountain," Lolly grabbed Ned's hand.

"It's challenging, you know. I don't think you're dressed for it," said Ned.

"Let's try. We can stop if it gets too rough. The view of the valley is so beautiful from up there."

"I remember. My father brought me here about six years ago. We made it to the top, but it wasn't easy," he said. "It was dangerous and took all day. Why don't we walk the railroad track to the ramshorn trestle? It's going to be dark soon, anyway."

"That's a good idea. We can climb the mountain some other time." She felt like an idiot. She'd never climbed the mountain at all. Her father never permitted her to go, even with a group, when she had the opportunity. She had no idea it was so treacherous.

"Let me show *you* something," Ned said.

Lolly followed Ned along the railroad track to the trestle. He helped her down the steep incline until they found the branch of Cain Creek that flowed under the bridge. They found themselves in one of the narrow valleys surrounded by ridges, one higher than the next. A waterfall flowed into the creek from one of the hills, and the verdant scenery was breathtaking. They could see the base of the sandstone mountain in the distance.

"What do you think?" Ned asked.

"It's unbelievable. I'm speechless," Lolly said. "I've never been under the bridge."

"We need to get back. It's getting dark."

Ned took her hand and pulled her up the steep incline to the track. They stood on the bridge and watched the setting sun paint the sky's canvas with hues of bright orange, yellow, and blue.

"I've never seen such a beautiful sky," Lolly said. "Will you come back here with me sometime?"

"Sure, I'd be glad to."

The hot summer day turned to darkness, and the Roadster traveled at a much slower pace since light from the side oil lamps was limited. Lolly didn't want the night to end. As they drove to the Clair farm, Ned rested his head on the leather seat and closed his eyes.

She pulled onto the long drive to the Clair farm and noticed a few lights in the main house while the bunkhouse was dark. As he slept, she gazed a few moments at his handsome face. His tweed cap covered his mop of longish dark hair. Ned's skin was flawless, and his chiseled facial features were most attractive. The man was rugged magnificence. "We're here," she said.

Ned stirred and opened his eyes. "I was tired, I guess. By the way, I enjoyed the scenic route."

"So, did I, Ned. Goodnight," Lolly said, hoping he would ask her to stay awhile.

"Wait. Stay a few minutes. It gets lonely around here, and I miss conversation with someone my age."

Lolly's heart skipped a beat. She turned off the engine and acted as if she was pondering the invitation. "Only for a few minutes." She got out of the car, took off her hat, and threw it on the leather seat. He led her to the bunkhouse and put on some coffee.

"Ned, I'm determined to find out who took Rachel from us," Lolly said. "Do you think it's James?"

"Sheriff Crow still thinks it is, but I don't," he said. "I want to conduct an investigation myself, but Sheriff Crow has the area at Cain Creek cordoned off with a 'no trespassing' sign and barricades."

"We should start a private investigation," Lolly began, "I have ways of finding out information about everyone in the community." She noticed his eyes filling with tears.

Ned cleared his throat. "We have to be discreet. I also have resources, but we must work together. There can't be any uncertainty if we find the bastard."

"I'll start checking on my end, and if I find anything you should see, I'll bring it over here. Agreed?" Lolly asked. "Has James been charged with murder?"

"Not yet, but I expect he will be any day."

After the coffee, Lolly got up from the crude farm table. "Thanks for letting me tear you away today."

They walked to the Roadster, and Lolly began to unfold the open top to cover the moist leather interior.

"I'm glad you drove by. It was a good time." Ned bent down and kissed her cheek. "I'll crank the engine."

The Alabama humidity was thick, but all she could think about was Ned McClure and that unexpected kiss. She got in, and the engine cranked with one turn.

On her way home, Lolly touched her cheek where he kissed her. Working so close with Ned on the investigation was a good idea.

CHAPTER 17

THE INVESTIGATION

From the day of Rachel's death, Ned's top priority was to find her killer, with or without the help of the sheriff. With Lolly's help, he hoped they could open a new chapter in the investigation. He planned to stop by Serenity Farm daily in hopes of seeing Rachel's image again and speaking to Dandy. He was restless and run-down from lack of sleep. He had begun to wonder if he'd imagined the vision of Rachel and even Dandy. His shaky emotional state and his general well-being were causing him concern.

Noble had instructed him to hire farmhands for the fall harvest. This year he would suggest to his boss the Clair farm was large enough to hire one year-round farmhand in addition to himself. Three apple orchards, a one-acre cotton field, and spring planting could keep two men employed for an unlimited period. It saddened him to see Ada's vegetable garden go to seed, but he could handle no more alone. Noble had become feeble and forgetful since his daughter's murder, while a lethargic Ada barely cared for Josie. She never ventured out of the house with her granddaughter. Ned had no legal rights to the child, and if he mentioned any concern about the child's care to anyone, Josie would be taken to an orphanage. He decided to visit the Clairs' before going to town.

Ned knocked on the front door of the main house. When he heard no sounds from within, he knocked again. No answer. Perhaps Noble was outside in the back, but he found no one. He tried the back door, but it was locked. He peeked through the open curtains of the kitchen window. There was Noble, Ada, and little Josie having lunch at the simple dining table. He knocked on the back door again. They didn't acknowledge the knock. There was no conversation between them, and Josie sat on Ada's lap as she spoon-fed the baby. Ned banged on the door. He watched as Noble got up and walked to the door.

The door opened to an overwhelming stench. "Mr. Clair, is everything in order here?"

"Yes, why do you ask?"

"May I come in?"

Noble backed away and gestured to Ned. "Sure."

Ned had never seen the main house in such a deplorable condition. The foul odor from old food, soiled diapers, and death clung to the kitchen. The decaying body of Christobel, Rachel's cat, lay in the corner. The heat from the scorching summer temperatures had ripened the air. "How long has Cristobel been dead, Noble?"

"A day or two, I think. The cat wasn't old, and in my opinion, it died of a broken heart. Christobel stopped eating," Noble said.

"Why has she been in the corner for so long? Don't you smell death?"

Noble didn't answer.

"I'll bury her by the barn," said Ned. "Then I'll be back. Don't lock the door. Do you hear me?"

Ned grabbed a cloth and picked up Rachel's beloved Christobel. The unfortunate animal was skin and bones. He lay her on the ground and retrieved a shovel from the barn. He dug a nice sized hole, wrapped the cloth around the cat and placed her inside. After replacing the dirt, he found two twigs to fashion a cross. Tears fell on the small mound as he put the makeshift cross at the head of the grave. "Rachel, I'm sorry she had to die like this, but I'm glad she's with you again."

Ned walked back to the house to find the back door locked. He pounded on it as he did before.

"Damn it, Noble! Answer the door," he yelled. The door slowly opened.

"Ned, what are you doing here? Glad to see you, boy," Noble began, "Is something the matter?"

Ned's heart broke again. "No sir, I'm going into town. Do you need anything?"

"No, I don't think so."

Ned pushed his way into the house. "Where are Mrs. Clair and Josie?" He feared for the child.

Noble walked to the parlor and found his favorite chair. "Ada's putting the baby to bed."

"I'll see you later then," said Ned. He peeked into Rachel's bedroom where Ada rocked Josie. The baby was asleep in her grandmother's arms.

Lolly used her hatpin and opened the door to her father's library. She looked under the rug for the key to the file cabinet, but it wasn't there. *Had he gotten wise to her?* She always left his medical files as she found them; with not one paper out of place. Rachel's file might shed light on the last week of her life. It was a long shot, but imperative to her part of the investigation.

It had been two days since she'd seen Ned. The urge to drive to the Clair farm was strong. "No, he has to come to me. Chasing him won't help," she muttered.

Almost dusk, Lolly walked outside and sat on the front porch. Though bored, as usual, she basked in the beautiful late afternoon. She decided to take a walk, but instead of taking a right on Cherry Street to town, she turned left toward the Clair farm. A few horse-drawn buggies and motor cars passed her, but Coal Springs was quiet for the most part.

Lolly found the branch marking the path to Cain Creek. She took the trail to the overgrown brush, evidence of the struggle that resulted in Rachel's death still visible. Lolly swiped angrily at the unwanted tears. Some markings remained to designate the crime scene, but in her opinion, the markings eliminated a lot of areas that could hold possible evidence. Lolly began to look under branches, inside bushes, even markings on trees. She checked the barely visible shoeprints inside the isolated area. *What good are they? I can't even make them out.*

With nightfall approaching, her amateur investigation would have to wait until tomorrow. There had to be a multitude of clues in the now tainted scrubland that held so many fond memories for her.

Lolly broke through the lush greenery leading to the road, turned right, and headed back to her house. As she passed Serenity Farm, she noticed dim lights in a few of the upstairs windows. She had never paid much attention to the dilapidated property. She knew it was vacant since Ned's family left Coal Springs. Who owned it now? She shrugged and continued to walk. It was getting quite late.

"Lolly!" Ned called from the direction of the Clair farm. "What are you doing here?"

She jumped with a start, then blushed. "You startled me. Taking an evening walk. What about you?"

"Heading to Crabtree's to see if any new flyers for farmhands have been posted. Care to join me?"

"Okay." Lolly's face continued to blush and was grateful it was too dark for Ned to see. "I passed your farm and saw lights in the windows."

Ned stopped. "You did? That's odd. No one lives there."

"Maybe it was the owner. Do you know who bought Serenity Farm?" Lolly asked.

Ned was surprised. "Your father. You didn't know?"

She felt sick. "No, I didn't. There's a lot about my father I don't know, it seems."

Lolly remained quiet as they walked the dusty road to Crabtree's. Her father was a bundle of surprises. What else was he hiding from her?

The usual collection of ne'er-do-wells congregated outside the mercantile. When the rowdy bunch saw Ned and Lolly, all eyes remained on them.

One of the men in the small group silenced the rest. "You're making the rounds, aren't you Ned?"

"Meaning what, Ben?" Ned asked.

"Meaning you get to mess around with the pretty ones," a drunken Ben Smalley taunted.

The men eyeing her made Lolly uncomfortable. When she noticed Ned ignoring them, she did the same.

"Good, Issac's flyer is still here. He worked hard for us last year," Ned said as he reached for another on the board. "Hmm, I don't recognize the other names on the flyers. Mr. Clair put me in charge of hiring this year."

As they walked from the mercantile toward the Hanes house, the men shouted obscenities and whistled.

"Did you notice who was shouting the loudest?" Lolly asked. "Mr. Foley. He and my father work side by side on the church budget. I hate this town."

"Ignore them," said Ned. "Keep walking."

After a few minutes, Lolly spoke. "Ned, I went to the clearing by the creek a little while ago. I don't think the sheriff is on the right track with his investigation. He's missing evidence that isn't roped off. There must be something outside the boundaries."

"He's sure James is guilty, so he thinks his investigation is over. He hasn't questioned any of the witnesses James saw at Crabtree's that night either."

"Maybe we should question them," Lolly suggested. "Do you have the names?"

"No, I think that should come up at the trial if there is one," he began. "Anyway, we might scare off the son-of-a-bitch."

"Will you meet me at the creek tomorrow around six?" she asked.

Ned opened the gate to Serenity Farm and found no lights in the windows. Lolly must have been mistaken. He felt the cloth-covered watch brooch in his pocket and opened the front door. The house was empty, and nothing had changed since his last visit two days before. He climbed the steps and went to the secret compartment in his parent's room. The velvet box was there, and he opened it. Inside lay another piece of paper on the same white parchment and written in the same beautiful script.

My dearest, the light is nearing, and all will be clear to you soon.

Your concerns are warranted and must be realized.

My love is with you always.

Ned's hand shook as he read the note. "Rachel, are you here?" The white flash of light sparked in the mirror. He turned to find the transparent form of Rachel Clair standing before him.

"Ned, keep my note close to your heart. What I say is true."

"Which part? I seem to be struggling with so many things; help me, please."

"Stay on the path of truth. You and Lolly will find your way."

At that moment, Ned heard a cat's meow. He looked around and saw nothing. When he looked back at Rachel, Christobel purred in her arms.

"I knew she was with you," he said. "I'm concerned about your folks."

"You are justified in your concern. You'll know what to do," Rachel said as she faded in the darkness.

"Rachel, don't go. I miss you so." Ned dropped to his knees and sobbed.

CHAPTER 18

LOOKING FOR EVIDENCE

James Cason was officially charged with the murder of Rachel Clair Cason. Ned saw the headline on the front page of the local county newspaper at Crabtree's. The arraignment would be at the county courthouse in Oden, on August nineteenth.

Ned hated James but didn't want an innocent man to hang for a crime he didn't commit. There had to be a way to delay the arraignment, or at least the trial. He needed to see the sheriff.

"I know James didn't commit the murder," Ned said as he walked into the sheriff's office.

"How do you know this?" Crow didn't look up from his paperwork. "We'll find out at the arraignment if the case ends up going to trial," he said, looking up at Ned. "Why is it you're defending the man?"

"There must be more evidence," Ned began. "Have you given the area by the creek a thorough inspection?"

The sheriff took off his spectacles. "It's my job to conduct a thorough investigation. Now, go on about your business and leave the case to me. I don't have time to conduct a wild goose chase."

It was a waste of time talking to the close-minded jackass. Ned had to meet Lolly at the creek in hopes of finding a clue, something there to shed light on the case. He left the sheriff's office and almost ran into Ben Smalley.

"I read about the charge against James," said Ben. "It doesn't surprise me one bit. Every night at the boarding house, I heard that poor girl crying, trying to reason with her husband. He wasn't nice to her. It upset my Vera terribly."

"Yes, sir." Ned didn't want to discuss Rachel, life at the boarding house, or the charge against James. He hurried past Ben on his way to meet Lolly.

It took Ned five minutes to reach the branch to the path. A yellow marker had been tied to it so the investigators could find their way to the crime scene.

Lolly was already there. "I haven't touched anything. I waited for you. I also brought a leather satchel just in case we find anything."

"Good," Ned said. "Let's take a look where the brush is bent and broken." He felt as if they were desecrating a grave. Rachel's precious life had ended there, and the overgrown brush might be hiding important information that could implicate the unknown bastard. Rachel implied it wasn't James, so they had to find something to prove it.

"I believe you when you say it wasn't James," said Lolly. "Why I don't know, but that's the reason we're here. Let's start under that huge wisteria vine next to the thick brush. That's where Rachel and I used to take our clothes off before we went swimming."

They were careful as they lifted each branch and sifted through the concealing covering of dry leaves. They checked the bark on trees and deep inside the bushes entangled in kudzu and old vines.

"Watch for poison ivy," Lolly said. "It's everywhere." She pulled on her lambskin gloves for protection.

"Lolly! Look here," Ned shouted. He found Rachel's shoes and stockings underneath the large privet. After almost four months, kudzu almost covered them completely. Lolly reached under and pulled out the ivory pumps, then the matching hosiery.

She began to cry. "These were her favorite shoes." She wiped them off with a cloth. "She loved them because they matched all of her summer dresses."

Ned wiped his eyes. "I remember these were the shoes and stockings Rachel wore that day," he said. "Her legs were bare when I found her."

"Are you sure?" Lolly placed them in the satchel and clasped it closed.

"I'm sure."

"You loved her very much, didn't you?"

"Yes, I did." He saw the change in Lolly's facial expression. Her furrowed brow and the unmistakable look of disappointment surprised him. "You knew that."

"Come on, let's keep going," Lolly said, brushing off Ned's response. "We have more ground to cover before it gets dark."

Lolly would have to wait until Ned's feelings for Rachel began to subside, no matter how long it took. Her love for him was alive and strong, not dead and buried.

Though dusk and hard to see, the two continued to explore the surrounding vegetation of the crime scene. But other than finding the shoes and stockings, they had no luck. This time.

Lolly kept the satchel and walked home alone in the dark. There were people around and a murderer on the loose, but as she passed Serenity Farm, her thoughts shifted to lights burning in the upstairs windows. It could be her father in there since he owned the property. But what would he be doing in the old house and why did he buy it in the first place?

Her curiosity forced her to open the old rusty gate. Lolly found gnarly vines and weeds taller than she was. Not knowing the clear paths to walk, she found herself running into overgrown bushes and tripping over old garden boulders. The dim firelight from the windows and the partial moon were the only sources of light she had. Once to the back door, Lolly held tight to the short railing, climbed a few steps, and stepped in what she assumed to be the kitchen. Placing the satchel on the floor, she fumbled around for a lantern. The flat surfaces were full of dust, but she managed to find a box of matches, then a candle. Lolly wasn't sure if she should light it or leave.

She stayed and lit the candle. The deserted kitchen was filthy, and she heard rodents scurrying inside the walls. Old newspapers were scattered about in the parlor along with whiskey bottles, crates and old blankets piled on the floor. Suddenly, a burst of cold air came from the staircase, and she gasped as her candle went out. She returned to the kitchen and grabbed the matches.

Lolly stood at the bottom of the stairs and looked up to the second floor. She expected the dim light from upstairs would guide her way, but now the second floor was dark. After relighting the candle, the rotten steps became visible. Sidestepping each disintegrating part, Lolly stopped and looked in each bedroom from a perch on the top step. The lantern cast enough light to make it clear no one was there, and no odor from burned lights was detected. *Had she imagined the lights from the road?*

She made her way down the steps. How could the lamplight be a product of her imagination? Once at the bottom of the stairs, she had the eerie feeling someone was watching her. Her hand shook as she blew out the flame. Lolly hurried out of the house and left the property knowing one sure thing; Serenity Farm was haunted, or the murderer was hiding out there.

CHAPTER 19

FACING THE TRUTH

When Ned returned to the Clair farm from Cain Creek, he tapped on the front door of the main house. The light was on in the parlor, so he knew Noble was home. Ned knocked again. Noble's odd behavior earlier caused marked concern, and he was worried about Josie.

"Noble! Open the damn door!" There was a fire burning in the fireplace, and it was August. Something was wrong. He ran to the back of the house and found no light coming from the kitchen window, and the door was locked.

"Come on, Noble," Ned muttered to himself as he banged on the door. Finally, he looked for something to break the window. Finding a mop, he pushed the handle through the glass and climbed into the kitchen.

"Noble!" Ned shouted. "Ada, where are you?" All he heard were Josie's cries in Rachel's bedroom. *Oh, God, let her be all right.* Ned followed the cries to find Ada on the floor in the corner of the room, rocking the child back and forth. Josie began to scream as her grandmother clasped her hands tighter around the little girl. Ned walked closer.

"No!" Ada shouted. "You can't take her."

"Ada, let me have Josie," Ned whispered. "She's hungry and needs to be changed."

"No, this is my daughter, Rachel, and no one will take her away again," Ada said in a stern voice.

Ned cleared his throat. His voice caught when he said, "Ada, this is Rachel's daughter, Josie." He couldn't hold back his emotion. "Allow me to take her for a few minutes. She needs food." Ned reached for the child, and Ada reluctantly gave her up. "I'll bring her back soon."

He had to get Josie out of the house, but where could he take her? She was thirteen months old and still a baby. He didn't know how to take care of a baby. Ned went to the front door and noticed Noble asleep in his chair. When he walked over to nudge him, he discovered Noble's body stiff and cold. He had died sitting in front of the blazing fireplace. Ned let out a deep sigh and closed his eyes. He needed to put out the flames, but how could he with Josie in his arms? The little girl continued to cry, and Ned knew nothing about quieting a baby.

The heat in the room was unbearable. Before leaving, Ned found a large vase of wilted wildflowers on the dining table and doused the fire with the remaining water. He went back to the bedroom to find Ada hadn't moved from the corner. With hands folded in her lap, she sat with no expression. Ned heard faint mumbling but couldn't make out her words. Josie cried louder as she reached for her grandmother. Ada wasn't fazed.

Grabbing what supplies he could find for Josie, Ned held tight to the child and lay her on the bed and changed her soiled diaper. The child's skin had blistered from chapping and looked almost blood red. He hoped the supplies he grabbed were the right ones. Not knowing if the cloth piece he grabbed was an actual diaper or not, he wrapped it crudely around the child's bottom then pinned it closed. Josie quieted some but needed food. What did she eat?

His first thought was Lolly. She might know, at least her father would. It took two hands to saddle the new horse, so he carried Josie and rushed to the Hanes' home.

Lolly heard a faint knock on the front door. "Sally, will you answer the door, please?"

"Yes, ma'am," the middle-aged white maid replied.

When Lolly heard Ned's voice and a baby crying, she hurried to the foyer.

"Ned, what's the matter?" she asked. "Why do you have Josie?"

"Lolly, I need help. She's starving, I think. I tried to change her diaper, but it's a bad job."

"Sally, please find Daddy and warm some milk!" Lolly said. "Ned, give her to me. What's happened?" Lolly took Josie and tried to calm her.

"Ada has gone crazy, the baby has been neglected, and I found Noble dead in the parlor."

Lolly gasped. "Oh, God. What can we do?"

"What's going on here, Ned?" Dr. Hanes asked as he walked into the foyer. He glanced at Lolly, holding Josie and looked back at Ned.

"Like I told Lolly, Noble Clair is dead, and Ada's mental capacities are gone," Ned took a deep breath, exhaled then wiped the sweat from his brow with his sleeve. "This is Rachel's baby. I don't know the last time she's eaten. Earlier in the day, I think. The skin around her rear-end needs medical attention."

"Lolly, take the child to my office so I can examine her. Sally, mash some of the leftovers from supper," Dr. Hanes instructed.

Lolly gestured for Ned to follow. "I'll keep Josie as long as needed," she said. "I have Sally to help me." She tried to soothe the crying child.

"Good, that eases my mind," Ned said.

As Lolly held Josie, Dr. Hanes managed a quick check of her throat, ears, and heartbeat. When the doctor lay the child on the examining table, the makeshift cloth diaper fell off, exposing irritated, broken skin, inflamed, red rash, and numerous blisters. When the doctor touched Josie, the baby screamed in pain.

"This child's diaper hadn't been changed in a few days," Dr. Hanes said. "The only way to treat the skin is to let her stay natural, and she should be fine in a few days." The doctor checked her abdomen, back, legs, and feet. "She is malnourished and dehydrated. Do you have anyone to care for her?"

"I'm taking Josie, Daddy. She'll stay here with Sally and me," Lolly stated. "That way, you can check her daily." Her father nodded his head in agreement.

"Ned, what about Ada and Noble?" the doctor asked. "Let's get the sheriff and ride out there."

"It's not good, Dr. Hanes," said Ned.

"We'll take the Roadster, Lolly. We don't have time to saddle Tony and take the carriage," Dr. Hanes said. "Do you know how to drive it, Ned?"

"I think so," Ned answered. "I've read up on the Model T, and I watched Lolly once."

Dr. Hanes cranked the engine on the first try. Ned eased the car out of the garage and onto the main road. "I think Noble died of a stroke or heart attack. That's just speculation, but he was acting strangely earlier today," he began, "that, and worry over Josie's care, prompted my visit tonight."

"Strange in what way?"

Ned explained Christobel's decaying body and the filth in the house. "After burying Christobel, Noble had no idea I'd been there fifteen minutes before or that the cat had died," he said. "I left the house this afternoon with Josie sleeping in Ada's arms," he said. "But I felt the need to check on the baby tonight."

"Good thing. It sounds as if Noble was suffering from 'senile dementia' which is a cognitive brain impairment and Ada is in emotional shock," said Dr. Hanes. "No doubt brought on by Rachel's death."

"Everything changed when Rachel died. Noble became an empty shell of a man and left the running of the farm up to me. That behavior doesn't befit his character."

Ned and Dr. Hanes entered the sheriff's office and explained the nature of the visit.

"I'll get my hat. Let's go," Sheriff Crow said. "You two follow me."

Ned parked the car in front of the main house dreading going inside. Smoke billowed out of the chimney. "I put that fire out before I left!" He hurried out of the car and ran to the front door. It was still locked. "Ada, open the door!"

After two tries, Sheriff Crow busted the door down. Ned went in after the sheriff and found Ada stoking the fire in the fireplace.

"Noble loves his fire," she said. "Somehow it went out, so I'm making sure he stays warm. He feels a little cold to me." Ada continued to stoke the raging fire. "I'm glad you came to visit. Rachel isn't home to help me with refreshments. She is constantly with Lolly."

Ned closed his eyes and lowered his head. He glanced over at Dr. Hanes. The doctor shook his head and looked at the sheriff.

"Mrs. Clair, what happened to Noble?" Sheriff Crow asked.

"He's sleeping, that's all. We had supper. He always falls asleep after a good supper." The sheriff looked over at Ned. "You know them better than anyone; how should we approach this?"

"Ada, come with us to the doctor's house," Ned began, "he invited you over for coffee and dessert. We won't bother Noble since he's sleeping so well."

"How nice, Justus. It's been a long time," Ada said. "How is Martha? I visited her many times. We talked about our babies constantly since they were so close in age."

"She's fine, Ada," Dr. Hanes said in an irritated manner and proceeded to examine Noble.

Ned noticed how uneasy the doctor became. He took Ada's arm and guided her to the car.

"Do I know you?" she asked.

"Yes, ma'am, I'm Ned McClure."

"Oh, yes. How is your mother? I don't see her much anymore," Ada said. "The only time I see Leona is in the springtime when she tends to her garden. I used to visit her when you were small, and I always brought Rachel."

"I don't remember," said Ned.

"I guess you were too young," she said. "After a while, your mother and father never saw anyone. I always wondered why. They are such lovely people."

Sheriff Crow and Dr. Hanes emerged from the house and walked to the car.

"Ned, take Mrs. Clair to the doctor's house. I'll see you there."

"Justus, I hope Martha is expecting me since I haven't seen her for such a long time," Ada called out as her head popped through the open space above the car door.

Ned waited for the distracted doctor. "Are you going to crank the engine, or am I?"

CHAPTER 20

A PAINFUL GOODBYE

"I haven't been here in so long, Justus," Ada said as she walked into the parlor of Dr. Hanes' home. "Where's Martha?"

"She'll be down directly," Dr. Hanes answered. "I'll be back in a moment."

When Ned joined her, he found Ada walking around the room and glancing at each framed photograph. Her hands were clasped behind her back as she bobbed her head up and down to see the displayed images on each table and larger ones hanging on the walls.

"See anyone you know?" Ned asked.

"Oh, yes," she answered. "Mostly Martha's daughter, but my Rachel is in one or two."

"Which are the ones with Rachel?"

Ada pointed to three. Ned recognized Rachel right away in only one. She must have been five years old, her blonde hair was worn down, and a large white bow sat on the crown of her head. She wore a fancy white dress and sat next to Lolly on the front porch of the doctor's home. Flowers surrounded the porch, and Rachel held a small bouquet.

"She was lovely," Ned said as he felt his eyes fill with tears.

"She is lovely."

Lolly walked into the room, and Ned turned away to hide his emotion.

"Hello, Mrs. Clair," Lolly said. "Sally is bringing the coffee and dessert. So glad you could come."

"Where's your mother? I want to see her," Ada demanded.

Ned watched Lolly's smile fade. He piped up and said, "She's out of town, Ada. The doctor told me a few minutes ago."

Sally came in with a sparkling silver coffee service and tray holding a plate of cookies, porcelain cups, and saucers. Ada smiled as she took a shortbread cookie and placed it on a lace-trimmed napkin. Lolly poured the coffee and gestured for Ned to sit down.

"The little bundle you left earlier is working out beautifully, Ned. I put it upstairs in my room so nothing would bother it. I'll check it in a moment. Would you like to join me?" Lolly asked.

Ned shot a puzzled look her way and then caught on. "I'll wait until tomorrow. No need to bother it tonight."

"This has been so nice; please tell Martha I'm sorry I missed her," Ada said as she placed her cup on the tray. "I need to go home and tuck Rachel into bed."

Ada stood then Ned. "Let me check on the Roadster," he began, "it should only take a minute." Ned slightly bowed and left the room. He was sick inside. Ada Clair's mind was crumbling right in front of him. He walked outside and found the sheriff talking to Dr. Hanes.

"Ned, it looks like Noble had a massive stroke and died instantly," said the doctor. "Does Ada seem any better?"

"No, the same. Ada still talks about the things that happened twenty years ago as if they happened yesterday."

"She can stay here tonight, but tomorrow she'll have to be admitted to a hospital in Birmingham," Dr. Hanes said. "The sheriff is making arrangements for Noble to be taken from the house and readied for burial."

"What type of hospital?" Ned asked.

"The Hillman Hospital for observation," he said. "She needs professional help right now."

"Well, then, I'll stop by tomorrow morning to check on Josie and Ada," Ned said as he started down the steps.

"Ned, wait!" Lolly said as she ran out the front door, "I was trying to tell you the baby ate well and is sleeping soundly in my bed. I think she'll be fine."

"I'm glad and thank you for helping out. I didn't know where else to turn." Ned tipped his hat. "I'll see you tomorrow."

When Lolly turned to go back inside, Ada stood in the doorway.

"I'm ready to go home now," she said.

"How would you like to stay with me tonight?" Lolly asked. "You'll have a nice room, and Sally will call us to breakfast in the morning at seven."

"No, I want to go home, but thank you," Ada said in an irritated tone of voice. "Rachel needs me."

Lolly didn't know what to do. How could she keep the woman at the house? Then it dawned on her. Josie was the answer.

"Rachel's here, Mrs. Clair, and sleeping upstairs." Lolly hated to deceive Ada, but there was no other way.

"She is? I want to tuck her in."

Lolly took Mrs. Clair's arm and led her up the ornate staircase. When they entered Lolly's room, Josie lay sleeping in the large tester bed. The gaslights were burning low, and Ada couldn't see much but the outline of the baby's form and the blonde curls.

"Oh, she's sleeping so soundly. I won't bother her. Isn't she the most beautiful baby you've seen?" Ada asked.

"Yes, she is," Lolly whispered. "You can sleep next to her." Ada smiled and removed her soot spattered dress. She left on her chemise and bloomers and unrolled her stockings and placed them in each leather pump. She climbed into bed and rested her head on the pillow next to Josie. Lolly retrieved a blanket and extra pillow out of her cedar chest and tried to sleep in a chair next to the bed. She was uncomfortable but wouldn't let Josie out of her sight.

Lolly awoke with the sun shining in the window. She looked at the mantel clock; it was seven o'clock. Josie and Ada were still sleeping. Before the baby woke up, Lolly ran to the water closet down the hall. She heard Josie talking in bed and hurried to take her downstairs before Ada realized the baby wasn't Rachel.

"Come on, Josie, let's go downstairs," Lolly whispered. Josie saw Ada and reached for her. "We'll let her sleep; she's so tired." Not knowing if she should wake Ada, Lolly went with her instinct and took Josie downstairs.

"Sally, I need your help," called Lolly. Josie was dry, but what about later? Her father said to keep her rear end naked, but was she to tinkle anywhere?

"Yes, ma'am?" Sally appeared in an instant.

"How can we keep this baby dry all day? Daddy said to keep her natural."

"Let's see how her rash is faring," Sally said.

They placed the baby on Dr. Hanes' examining table. The inflammation and rash looked a little better.

"We should coat her bottom in petroleum jelly. That will nourish the skin and take the soreness away," Sally said.

"Maybe I should take her to the water closet," said Lolly.

"Let's coat her first; then I'll take her."

Lolly carried Josie to the water closet and sat her down. After a few minutes, Josie had finished and smiled. "Good girl!" Lolly said.

After breakfast, Lolly wiped Josie's mouth and saw Ada standing in the doorway.

"It's my job to feed Rachel," Ada said. "Not yours."

"You were sleeping, and I didn't want to wake you."

Ada, once again wearing her soot-covered dress, walked around the table and sat next to Josie. "This is such a pretty room," she said with a smile. "I always liked it. Martha and I fed you and Rachel lunch in here many times." Ada looked at Josie, then Lolly. "This isn't Rachel! Where's Rachel?" She got up and tried to run out of the room. Dr. Hanes caught her as he entered the dining room.

"What is the problem?" he asked.

"Where's Rachel, Justus? This baby isn't Rachel!" Ada cried out and began to sob.

"Now, now. Rachel left early this morning. Don't worry." Dr. Hanes put his arm around Ada and patted her shoulder, "She'll be back soon."

Lolly wondered why the woman couldn't snap out of this unhealthy condition. She wanted to shake Ada and tell her to get a hold of herself, but it became clear there was nothing anyone could do. Rachel's mother, Mrs. Clair, a woman she'd known all her life had given way to madness. Ada, Dr. Hanes, and Lolly sat in the dining room until Hillman's horse-drawn carriage arrived to take her to the hospital.

One woman and two men approached Ada and introduced themselves as Mrs. Culver, Dr. Weldon, and Mr. Lawler.

"Mrs. Clair, we're here to take you on a new adventure," Mrs. Culver said.

"What adventure? I have to go home," Ada replied. "My daughter will be back soon."

Lolly started to leave the room. She couldn't bear to witness Ada escorted to an ambulance, but her father gestured for her to stay.

"The gardens are in full bloom, and wild birds will eat right out of your hand," the nurse said.

"I have plenty of birds at home. My mother always lets me feed them."

Mr. Lawler glanced at Dr. Hanes, and he nodded his head, which assured the orderly the time was right to take her.

"Come with us, Mrs. Clair," said Mr. Lawler. "It's a beautiful day. The sky is bright blue, and the open-air carriage will allow you to see such wonderful things."

As Mr. Lawler took Ada's arm, Mrs. Culver held her hand and walked outside to the porch. They stopped to wait for Dr. Weldon.

"Will she be cared for properly?" Lolly asked.

"Yes. Mrs. Clair's case doesn't seem life-threatening or permanent," Dr. Weldon began, "but the death of her daughter triggered tremendous shock that has caused temporary hysteria."

"So, will she be coming home soon?" Lolly asked.

"That will be determined, but I believe so," he said. "Now, it will take time, and you may visit anytime."

"I'll walk you out, Doctor," Dr. Hanes said.

Lolly followed and stood on the porch. It was a beautiful day, but Ada Clair was leaving Coal Springs with assistance. As she walked to the ambulance holding Mrs. Culver's hand, there was no defiance or screaming, just the familiar soft-spoken voice. Ada's words were inaudible and directed to the nurse. Mr. Lawler helped Ada into the back of the carriage while Mrs. Culver followed. As they pulled away, Ada smiled and waved goodbye.

CHAPTER 21

LOLLY'S SEARCH

"There's something unseemly going on at the Hanes house," remarked spinster, Miss Janette Foley. She, her mother, Agnes, and two of the deacon's wives were attending the weekly Bible study at the home of Mrs. Gladys Crabtree.

"What do you mean?" Mrs. Edna Puckett asked. "That daughter of Justus Hanes takes up with anybody, so I'm not surprised."

Miss Janette pulled her chair in closer. "Well, I've seen Lolly Hanes and Ned McClure out together alone. And I don't mean just once."

"Really. What does it mean? I'm sure Justus has no idea," added Mrs. Arelia Pope. "He would never allow it."

"And another thing. Just the other day, I saw Ada Clair coming out of the Hanes house with two men and a woman," said Miss Janette. "The side of their carriage said Hillman Hospital."

"There's something to what Janette says," stated Mrs. Crabtree. "My Rufus saw Lolly and Ned on the Hanes porch with a baby, together. They were at the mercantile the other night and going into the woods together near Cain Creek. Yes, we need to talk to Justus," she said as she picked up her Bible. "The sin in our community since that Clair girl's situation is getting out of hand, and we must put an end to it."

"Ladies, before we get back to our lesson, let us pray for their wicked souls," Mrs. Pope said as she bowed her head.

ꟷ

Noble Clair's funeral was not well attended. The closed-minded community had turned their backs on his family because of Rachel and Josie, even though he followed their lead relating to Rachel's marriage. He was buried next to his daughter in the Coal Springs Church Cemetery with Reverend Bradshaw, Lolly, Dr. Hanes, and Ned the only ones in attendance. The somber atmosphere was also fueled by the possible murder trial of James Cason.

Ned had never felt more alone. With Noble dead and Ada away in Birmingham, he cleaned the main house and boarded it up. Issac would arrive the next day, so he also cleaned the bunkhouse.

He tied the new horse to the hitch in front of the mercantile, and snide remarks and obscenities about Lolly could be heard.

"New girlfriend, Ned? A baby so soon?" Laughter erupted, then quieted as old man Foley shouted, "How 'bout them woods, Ned 'ol boy? We know how you and the doc's girl sneak away."

What the hell are they talking about? Ned ignored them and found Issac.

"Right on time, as usual," Ned shouted over the loud voices. "I'm glad to see you. It's been a long year."

"I be sorry for all the pain you be goin' through, Ned," said Issac as they met in front of the store and shook hands. "That's mo than most folk could take."

"When Rachel was killed, my future died with her," said Ned. "Now we have to relive it all over again with the possible trial. But we can't keep Noble's crops from the market."

"No, and we sho won't," said Issac. "New hoss?"

"Yes, this is General Lee. We lost Old General seven days after Rachel."

"My, my. I hates to hear it," Issac shook his head and wiped his eyes with his sleeve. "But Mr. Clair sho like his generals,"

Issac said with a slight chuckle. "Don't you worry, Ned. Everything gon be okay."

As they passed the Hanes' house, Lolly waved from the porch. She held Josie and showed the baby how to wave.

"Let's stop for a minute, Issac," said Ned. "Lolly's keeping Josie now."

Lolly met them by the main road. "Hello, Ned." Josie smiled at Issac.

"This is Issac. He's helping me with the harvest again this year," said Ned.

Issac tipped his hat and nodded. "Ma'am."

"Hello, Issac." Lolly smiled. "I'm glad to know you."

"Listen, have you been back to Cain Creek since we were there last week?" Ned asked.

"No, but I'm going today," said Lolly as Josie laughed at Issac.

"I can't meet you today until six," Ned said.

On the way back to the Clair farm, Ned filled Issac in on the amateur investigation at Cain Creek. With the trial coming up, he hoped to have some evidence in time to vindicate James of Rachel's murder.

Issac seemed puzzled. "Why would you try to help that boy?"

"I know he didn't do it. He is a mean bastard, and I loathe the sight of him, but the timeline doesn't match up," he said as he squinted into the sun. "The truth will all come out if there is a trial." When General Lee turned onto the Clair property, Ned noticed a horseless carriage boasting the county insignia on the side. Who is this?

"Ned McClure?" the man in a dark suit asked.

"Yes."

"This is for you," the man said as he handed Ned a piece of paper.

"Issac Mosley?"

"Yassa."

"This is for you." The man handed Issac one as well. "Good day." He stepped up to sit in the carriage and drove away.

They had both been served a summons to appear in court on September 3rd, 1910, at the county courthouse in Oden, for the trial and prosecution of James Cason.

"There will be a trial, and it's next week, Issac," said Ned. "James must have pled, not guilty. Who knows how long we'll be away?"

"Well, I guess we better get to workin'," Issac replied. "How they know about me?"

"Probably from Ada's statement before the arraignment when James was charged with aggravated assault. She mentioned how you carried Rachel in the house that night."

Lolly hadn't mentioned to Ned about her experience at Serenity Farm. He might think she was crazy. And now with Ned tied up with the harvest, she decided to wait before she told him. But what if the murderer was hiding out there? She wasn't about to tell the worthless sheriff. For the time being, she would concentrate on the investigation, and go to Cain Creek after lunch while Josie was napping.

When she turned onto the marked path, Lolly noticed how some of the brush had been freshly trimmed back and leafless branches were exposed. Swimming in this part of the creek was prohibited since it was a major crime scene. *If the creek is closed off, who has permission to trim the foliage?*

Lolly walked a trail off the beaten path she and Ned hadn't the time to search. It ran parallel to the creek and had no markers identifying it as part of the crime scene. She slipped on her gloves and began to pull back branches and sift through dead leaves. After turning over almost every leaf on five or six bushes, she sat on the ground to rest. She looked around for more overgrown paths that looked disrupted. She pulled a jar of water out of her satchel and unscrewed the lid. As she took a sip, a shiny object on a path on the hill cast a glare from the sun and shone so bright she had to block it with her hand.

She crawled through the tangled kudzu vines hanging from a large oak tree. On the ground near the tree, she found a partially hidden silver snuff tin with worn initials engraved on the top. Was the first one a J or a D? Lolly couldn't make them out. While she studied the tin, a soft rustling sound diverted her attention.

The thick kudzu was dying away, but enough remained to conceal small rodents. Lolly remained still as a large cottonmouth slithered in her direction away from the creek. Lolly froze as it slid across her shoes and paused under the large oak five feet away. While she waited for the reptile to move, she spotted another item covered with leaves. From what she could see, it was an old "Bulwark" Cut Plug tobacco tin. Still frozen, she looked for a long stick to pick up. The snake didn't move.

Josie would be waking up soon, so Lolly had to quickly retrieve the tin. She saw a dead branch hanging from a nearby scrub tree. Reaching as far as she could, the tip was close enough to grab. Bringing it down caused a loud crackling sound which disturbed the quiet calm of the woods. Lolly looked for the snake, but it had slithered away.

Holding the branch as a defense in case the snake was camouflaged, Lolly stepped with caution to the green tin. She moved the greenery around it and found no snake. Relieved, she picked up the rusty tin. Wearing her gloves, she opened it to find five cigarettes and five matches. "Now we're getting somewhere."

Arriving at the Clair farm, Lolly saw Ned and Issac leading General Lee to the barn. The baskets on the buckboard looked full, so Lolly planned to stay long enough to show Ned the snuff box and cigarette case. Then she noticed the boarded-up windows on the main house.

"Ned," she shouted and waved. "I need to see you."

Issac took General Lee's reins. Ned waved and walked in Lolly's direction.

"So, you went ahead and closed the house," she said. "I don't blame you." Trying not to switch subjects too quickly, Lolly stated, "I went to Cain Creek this afternoon and found a few pieces of evidence," she began. "I hope they're significant." Lolly reached in the satchel and pulled out the tins.

"Where did you find these?" Ned asked as he took the silver one with the engraving.

"On the hill by the path that runs parallel to the water. It was by a tree. Can you make out the initials?"

"The first one looks like an I, but I can't make out the other two. May I keep the tin and study the initials?" Ned asked.

"Of course, we're in this together. Look at this one, too." She showed him the "Bulwark" tin with the cigarettes inside.

"Crabtree sells this brand of plug," Ned said. "Sometimes the tin is kept for other uses. This is great, Lolly."

"I hope it sheds some light on the case," she said. "It was hell retrieving the green one. I had a water moccasin as a partner." She chuckled. "Oh, by the way, I went to Serenity Farm the other night. I think it's haunted or someone is hiding out."

Ned quickly jerked his head and cut his eyes in her direction. "Why do you say that?"

Lolly was surprised at his reaction. "Lights were burning in the upstairs windows, but when I went in, they were out." She placed the "Bulwark" tin back in her satchel. "The place is dangerous and filthy. Gnarly vines and weeds were everywhere."

"You shouldn't go there alone. You might get hurt."

"I'm going right now. It's dark enough," Lolly said as she looked up to the sky.

"Wait, I'll go with you," he said.

"What about the baskets on the buckboard?" Lolly asked.

"Issac can start; I'll help him finish."

Lolly and Ned pulled in front of Serenity Farm. No lights shone from the windows, and the old gate was ajar. Nailed to a tree was a NO TRESPASSING sign.

"That was never here," Ned said before getting out of the Roadster. "Have you seen it before?"

"No, but it doesn't matter. I own the property, at least my father does," Lolly said. "Come on; let's go in." She handed Ned a house light and two 'D' batteries while keeping the candles and matches for herself. She was prepared this time.

Ned led the way through the cleared path to the backdoor. There were no gnarley vines or tall weeds obstructing the walk.

"What happened to the weeds and vines?" Lolly said. "I tripped and almost fell right about here." She pointed to where the old garden boulders had been. "The boulders are gone."

They proceeded to the back door and found it locked. "This door is never locked," said Ned.

Lolly bent down and found a long stick. "Break the window. I'll take responsibility for it."

After Ned shattered the window, they crawled through it and fell into the kitchen area. The floor had been swept, counters scrubbed, and the kettle began to boil.

"Well, well, my boy," called Dandy from the parlor. "Just in time for tea."

"Dandy, where have you been?" asked Ned. He noticed how Lolly's mouth dropped open.

"Here and there. I wanted to come back and check on the farm," Dandy said. "Did you see the collards? They're growing like weeds."

Ned took Lolly's arm and said, "This is Dandy Day. He worked for my parents here a long time ago."

"Hello, Dandy. Please forgive my surprise," she said, "but I was here a few nights ago, and the grounds were deplorable."

"That's what happens when I leave, no one takes care of the property," said Dandy. "I'm back for a little while now."

"Does my father know you're here? Did he permit you to stay?" Lolly wondered if the old man even knew her father.

"Your father has known me for years. He doesn't mind my being here because he doesn't know," Dandy answered with a chuckle.

Ned looked at Dandy, then Lolly. "I'm going to take her upstairs. She ought to see the property she owns."

"This house makes my skin crawl. It's haunted, I know it." Lolly grabbed Ned's arm and stuck close-by as he led her through the parlor.

The sudden burst of cold air blew Lolly's candle out. She screamed.

"Watch your step," said Ned as he guided them with the house light up the stairs. When they got to the top, Ned walked into his parent's room to the secret compartment. A note lay inside the velvet box.

"What is it?" Lolly asked.

"You'll see." He took out the note. It was for Lolly.

My dear one, do not be afraid. Your serenity and truth
are provided here. You and Ned will see clear,
and the path will come to an end. Then you will understand.
My love lives with you both.

As Lolly read the beautiful script, tears filled her eyes. "Is Rachel here?"

A quick flash came from the mirror as Lolly and Ned stood before it. In an instant, Rachel appeared in her flowing white gown and floral adornments.

"Rachel, I miss you so," said Lolly. "You are beautiful."

"Your findings will lead you to the truth. When that day comes, your new life will begin. So much love and happiness will be yours," Rachel answered.

"What do you mean?" Lolly asked as Rachel began to fade. "Wait! Don't go, please." She turned and sobbed into Ned's shoulder.

Ned smiled and said, "You see? We haven't lost her forever."

"But why didn't you tell me?" Lolly asked as she wiped her tears.

"Would you have believed me?"

CHAPTER 22

THE TRIAL OF JAMES CASON

Oden County Courthouse Oden, Alabama

It was raining on the third of September 1909. As thunderstorms pounded north-central Alabama, reporters stood by while Judge J.T. Greene entered the courtroom.

"All rise," the bailiff announced. "This is Case Number 19895. The State of Alabama versus James Cason.

Ned and Lolly sat with the spectators, which included the clique of the church elite. When James Cason walked in wearing leg irons and handcuffs, the devout women could be heard whispering and giggling. James was clean-shaven, and his dark hair well-groomed. He wore his familiar dark suit with a stiff starched tall collar and thin tie. He made eye contact with no one.

"While my courtroom is in session, I will not tolerate commotion of any kind," Judge Greene announced with disgust. "If you ladies have something to say, let's hear it or leave this room."

Ned thought of the many times James beat Rachel and hated him for it. He had been convicted of assault and battery against her and was paying for that crime in prison. Now he was on trial for her murder, but he was innocent. How could he bring himself to help a man like James?

"James Cason, you are on trial for the brutal murder of Rachel Clair Cason, and you have waived a jury trial. Let's proceed." Judge Greene announced.

James sat quietly as his public defender shuffled papers on the table and appeared to be unorganized.

"The prosecution will proceed with his opening statement," said the judge. "Mr. Comer, you may begin."

"Your Honor, this man is on trial for the murder of his wife, a young and lovely girl who had just become a mother. He is currently serving time for beating her numerous times to the point of near-death."

Ned watched James as the prosecutor explained each beating, the refusal to work, and the drunkenness. When he described the mortal blows, James put his head in his hands and cried.

The defense attorney, Sam Hastings, opened with the timeline of the fatal day, and how James couldn't have been in two places at one time. He had the witnesses to prove it, and they would be called to testify.

Ned whispered to Lolly, "Do you have the tobacco tins with you?"

"Yes, they're in my bag. Why?"

"When the judge dismisses court today, I want to find a jeweler here in town," he said. "Maybe he can make out the engraved initials on the silver one."

After the attorneys concluded the opening statements, the first witness for the prosecution was called.

"Ned McClure, please come forward," the bailiff said in a loud, deep voice.

Ned cleared his throat and proceeded to the front of the courtroom. On the way, he made eye contact with James, who quickly looked away.

"Place your left hand on the Bible, and raise your right. Do you swear to tell the truth, whole truth, and nothing but the truth?"

Yes, I do," Ned answered.

After Ned stated his name and occupation, the first question asked was from John T. Comer, the district attorney of Oden County.

His initial line of questioning pertained to Rachel's previous beatings from James. Ned recounted the details of the night she returned to the farm after sustaining a severe head injury.

"When was the first time you saw James Cason on the day in question, and how do you describe his demeanor?"

"Rachel and I were sitting under the oak tree in front of the Clair main house. We were playing with her daughter, Josie," he said. "It was around three o'clock when James walked down the drive. He wanted to speak to Rachel in private."

"Was he mad, aggravated, or the like?" Comer asked.

"No, he was civil, but she wouldn't speak to him alone," he began, "Rachel wanted me to stay." Ned's hands became sweaty and then rubbed them on his thighs. "He persisted; that's when I stepped in. He took a swing at me."

"Did you all have a physical fight?"

"Only one punch each. I told James I didn't want to fight with him," Ned said. "He was angry and left."

"Did he say anything when he left?" Comer asked.

He said, "This isn't over, Rachel." Ned added, "I don't know what that meant."

The next set of questions were about the timeline and when Ned found Rachel's body. Ned was forced to recall her injuries and repeat how he discovered her beautiful face beaten almost beyond recognition. Reliving the memory of that day caused his voice to break as he tried to describe her broken body.

"Thank you, that's all for now," Comer said.

"No questions at this time, Your Honor," said Sam Hastings, the public defender.

"The court calls Dr. Justus Hanes," the bailiff said in his bellowing voice.

Ned returned to his chair next to Lolly. The recollection of the injuries Rachel had suffered cut deep into his soul, and now the doctor would pour more salt in the open wound.

Dr. Hanes swore to tell the truth and gave Rachel's medical history, the nature of the injuries, and what part of the fatal attack caused her death.

As the doctor spoke, Ned's thoughts focused on Rachel's injuries and where each one was on her body. The previous blows from James had always been about her head and face. The bruises and the multiple broken bones didn't mesh with his past assaults.

Dr. Hanes's answers fell in line with Ned's observation. One thing the doctor brought to light was that James Cason was an average-sized man, but concluded after the post-mortem examination, a physically powerful person inflicted Rachel's mortal blow.

The last statement made by Dr. Hanes agitated the Coal Springs spectators and caused the judge to pound the gavel. "I will clear this courtroom if I don't have silence!"

The room quieted, and the doctor was dismissed with no more questions. Dr. Hanes now confirmed Ned's speculation, and he hoped the jeweler would be a significant player in the case.

"Court is adjourned until ten o'clock tomorrow morning," Judge Greene announced as he pounded the gavel.

"Thank goodness, I can't listen to anymore," said Lolly.

"Let's find a jeweler." Ned grabbed Lolly's arm and guided her out of the courtroom. "Where's Issac?" he asked as he looked around the crowded hallway.

"Ned!" Issac called. "Wait."

"Where have you been?" Ned asked.

"I be directed to the gallery. That the only place I can watch the trial," Issac said.

Ned took a deep breath and rolled his eyes. "Those damn bureaucrats. Let's eat lunch, then search for a jeweler."

"I hopes we find the man. The little gal didn't deserve to die that way," said Issac as he shook his head.

No longer raining, Ned found a bench in front of the courthouse where Lolly unpacked the lunch basket Sally had prepared. Ned and Issac insisted on standing while she spread out pimento cheese sandwiches, fruit, closed tins of potted meat, and white cake. Lolly served lemonade from a jar in glass cups the maid had provided.

The town of Oden was the county seat and built around the courthouse. The local shops, businesses, government building, and the grounds were considered Town Square. As Ned ate, he read the signs over each storefront. There were shops for ladies' clothing, men's attire, a bank, and a druggist. He didn't see a jeweler.

When two well-dressed local women passed, Ned stopped them. "Excuse me, is there a jeweler in town?"

"Yes, on the corner of Temple Street and Sixth Avenue," the attractive older one replied and winked. "We'll be glad to walk you there."

"That won't be necessary, but thank you," said Ned as he shot a glance at Issac.

"I think she want mo than a walk," Issac said with a laugh. "Don't worry, Miss Lolly didn't see a thing."

After lunch, Ned and Lolly walked through the open door of Webster's General Store. The store devoted one corner for two wooden display counters with glass sides and tops. Intricate rings, necklaces, and watch brooches lay showcased under glass as well as men's pocket watches, fobs, signet rings, and cufflinks.

"May I see the jeweler?" Ned asked a man standing behind the front counter.

"I'm Tom Webster, the owner, and jeweler," the man replied.

"Would you mind taking a look at this silver snuff-box?" Lolly took it out of her bag and removed the lace handkerchief wrapped around it. "We're trying to find the owner but can't make out the engraved initials."

Mr. Webster brought out his loupe and inspected the box.

"This box is old, and the initials have worn off for the most part, but I might be able to match what's left of them with the samples my customers used to choose from. Since I no longer offer to engrave here in the store, I still have this book of letter styles." He offered a thin booklet full of numerous letters of the alphabet in various sizes and typefaces.

"Do you see a match?" Lolly asked.

"This old script looks very close to one of the partial initials on the box," Mr. Webster said as he pointed to a beautiful calligraphic styled example. He brought the loupe close to his eye and compared the similarities. He examined each uppercase letter, then switched back and forth from the script to the silver box. After many long minutes, he said, "Yes, this seems to be the match for the first initial."

Ned leaned in as Mr. Webster pointed out the elegant swoops and extended curves of the calligraphic letter.

"See this design?" Mr. Webster ran his wrinkled finger across the matching typeface. "These symbols of the alphabet were drawn by hand, and each one has its distinguishing trait."

"In your expert opinion, what is the initial?" Ned tried not to sound too eager.

"If you two will compare the flourish of the extension, and how the calligrapher finished the letter with teardrops, you'll see the letter is a T," the old jeweler confirmed.

Ned looked at Lolly. "The initial T?" he asked. "Who could this be?"

Mr. Webster studied the next letter. "This initial in the center is almost worn completely off," he said. "I'll come back to that one." The jeweler focused on the last initial. "Again, by the looks of the extensions and teardrop detail, this is the letter B."

"We have a T and a B so far," said Ned as Mr. Webster concentrated on the center initial. "Can you make the last one out?"

"This one is difficult. There isn't much to decipher."

Ned tried to control his anxiety. He paced the floor then walked outside. Issac waved him over from across the street.

"Did y'all fine out the letters?" Issac asked.

"Not all. Mr. Webster is working on the last one."

After fifteen minutes, Lolly shouted, "Ned, Mr. Webster figured it out."

"As difficult as it was, I magnified the site of the initial and followed the indention of the original engraving needle with this little tool." He held up a sewing needle. "As before, the teardrops and extensions match the other letters. The center initial is an S."

"Hmm, T S B," said Lolly. "We still have a lot of ground to cover."

"You've saved us a lot of time, Mr. Webster," said Ned. "You don't know how much this helps."

"Thank you, Mr. Webster," Lolly said. "May we pay you for your time?"

"No, no," he answered. "My assumption is you're here for the trial. I hope this confirmation will help with your search for the owner of the box."

Lolly grabbed Ned by the arm and led him back to the town square to join Issac. "I don't know anyone whose name begins with T," she said. "What if the person doesn't live in Coal Springs?"

"He has to," Ned said with a determined look. "And I'll find him."

&

The trial resumed the next morning with Issac called as the first witness.

"Issac Moseley," the bailiff called.

Ned caught sight of Issac making his way through the gallery crowd and down the stairs. As he entered the courtroom, the bailiff looked around the room for the witness.

"Issac Moseley," the bailiff repeated.

"Here, sir," Issac said as he held up one hand.

"Where are you sitting?" Judge Greene asked.

"In the gallery, sir," he answered while standing in front of the witness stand.

"Make a note of this, you people. Mr. Moseley is a witness, and all witnesses will be seated with the spectators," the judge ordered. "We have no time for unnecessary delays." Judge Greene rubbed his forehead and shook his head "Proceed."

Issac took his oath on the Bible and sat down.

"Mr. Moseley, from earlier witnesses, you were quoted as saying, in so many words, that Rachel Clair Cason was beaten on the night you carried her inside Noble Clair's farmhouse. Is that true?" Mr. Hodges asked.

"Yessa," he replied.

"How do you know this?"

"I grow'd up with a daddy that beat my mama. I knows cuts and bruises from bein' beat. I be beat many a time my own self by my daddy," Issac said. "I be expert in that." Issac recollected the night in question, and the occasion when he observed James and Rachel in Crabtree's store with Josie. "He be mean to that little lady."

Ned glanced at James sitting at the defense table with no expression. After Issac stepped down from the witness stand, James continued to make no eye contact with anyone.

Lolly made room for Issac next to them with the spectators. Ned leaned over and nodded when Issac took his seat.

The next witness from Coal Springs was Ben Smalley. After being sworn in, Comer asked, "Mr. Smalley; you own the boarding house where the Cason's lived, do you not?"

"I do," he said.

"What comes to mind when you think of your lodgers, the Casons?"

"I only know Rachel, Mrs. Cason, cried most of the time, and I heard loud noises and yelling on many occasions. The behavior upset my wife, Vera," Smalley said. "My little girls would sometimes ask their mother to bring the baby to our room when the fights started."

"And did the baby come to your room?"

"Not much. My wife is too busy keeping up the boarding house and cooking for our lodgers," he said. "Mrs. Cason let my girls play with the baby when she was outside."

"Is your wife present in the courtroom, Mr. Smalley?" Comer asked.

"No, sir, she had to stay at home. It's harvest time, and our seasonal lodgers have checked in. She also didn't receive a summons."

Ned listened to Smalley and thought about how much harvesting he and Issac were missing. He needed to return to Noble's farm and hoped the defense wouldn't call him to testify, but Serenity Farm and the image of Rachel continued to fill his thoughts.

"Ned, the defense is calling you," Lolly whispered as she nudged his arm.

"Ned McClure," called the bailiff.

He walked to the witness stand and raised his right hand.

"You're still under oath, son," said Judge Greene.

"Mr. McClure, you don't like Mr. Cason much, do you?" Hastings asked.

That wasn't a question he expected. "No, I don't."

Hastings then asked, "Is it because you were in love with his wife?"

The full courtroom gasped, and a few of the church women waved their surprised faces with their folding fans.

"I won't deny it. I did love Rachel," Ned said.

The courtroom erupted in intense hostility. One man yelled, "He's just like his mother! He didn't care if Rachel had a husband or not!"

Ned cut his eyes in Joe Foley's direction. Foley led the religious hypocrites as they stood yelling obscenities and names at Ned.

"That outburst was uncalled for. Bailiff, remove that man from this courtroom!" Judge Greene ordered in disgust. "As for all the rest of you, I will not tolerate poor behavior in my courtroom."

The room fell quiet, and Sam Hastings resumed his questioning.

Ned's attitude never wavered. He was prepared for anything Hastings threw at him and was eager to answer.

"Did you feel hostile toward James Cason at any time before and after the marriage?"

"Yes." Ned waited for the next question from Hastings. "A few times."

"What were those times, Mr. McClure?"

Ned explained the hostility began the first day James Cason set foot on the Clair property two years before. He told how James implied sexual innuendo and made repeated snide remarks about Rachel to the other farmhands.

"What about the time after James Cason returned to Coal Springs after seven months away?" Hastings asked.

"James, it turns out, raped Rachel during the first harvest dance which resulted in pregnancy," Ned said.

The courtroom burst into loud accusations and finger-pointing. Some of the women from Coal Springs acted as if they would faint and fanned themselves wildly.

"I warned you, people. I will empty this courtroom," shouted the judge as he pounded his gavel. "Proceed, Mr. McClure."

"I hoped she'd reject him and marry me. Her parents intervened."

"Did they force her into the marriage?"

"Yes, they did."

The courtroom erupted again into another outburst.

"Clear this courtroom!" Judge Greene ordered. "Except for the witnesses."

In minutes, the spectator seats and gallery were cleared.

"Proceed." Judge Greene nodded to Sam Hastings.

"Mr. McClure, what brought on your further hostility toward Mr. Cason?" Hastings asked.

Ned recounted the visit to Dr. Hanes's office and how he'd seen Rachel's black eye and stitched lip. He explained in detail how the same night, she almost fainted from walking to the Clair farm due to a severe concussion. His testimony was consistent with Dr. Hanes and Issac's sworn testimonies.

"Mr. McClure, did you kill Rachel Clair Cason to get back at James Cason?"

Lolly gasped at the question. Issac stopped her from standing up with a 'wait-a-minute' hand motion before Ned answered the question.

"No, sir, I did not. I loved her." He blinked back tears.

"Thank you. I have no further questions for this witness," Hastings said.

"Court adjourned until tomorrow morning at ten o'clock." Judge Greene pounded his gavel and rose to leave.

"Judge Greene, may I have a word with you, sir?" Ned asked.

All other witnesses had left the courtroom except Dr. Hanes, Lolly, and Issac.

"Unusual, but I can't see any harm in it," the judge replied.

"Lawyers and Mr. McClure, follow me to my office."

When the judge opened the door to his office, he led the way and motioned for the men to sit down in three cushioned leather chairs. "What is it, my boy?"

"I have evidence that might change the course of this trial," Ned began, "my friend and I began our own investigation outside of the crime scene markers." Ned wouldn't show the tins unless the judge ordered it. "Your Honor, if you'll delay the trial two days, I think we can drop the son-of-a-bitch in your lap."

"Now, wait a minute, I thought you hated James Cason," said Comer. "Why are you trying to help him?"

"I despise him, but I think I can prove he's innocent of Rachel's murder," Ned said. "He was convicted of assault and will be in prison for a long time. I can't let what James was guilty of before condemn him for a crime he didn't commit."

Judge Greene thought for a moment. "I'll allow it since you're so adamant about helping someone you despise." When glancing toward the lawyers, he said, "Make sure all witnesses know of the delay."

ꟼ

Ned, Lolly, and Issac motored back to Coal Springs in the Roadster that afternoon and felt confident the criminal was someone in town that had a vendetta against James.

"Who could it be? Where do we go first?" Lolly asked. "We should be home in an hour or so."

"I needs to get to the farm. There be a lot of bad apples on the ground," said Issac. "An the cotton won't be a pickin' itself."

"Issac's right. We need to check on the farm. Lolly, meet me at Crabtree's at seven o'clock."

ꟼ

Lolly was happy to see Josie and excited to hear the baby had learned to clap her hands while she was away. After playing with Josie on the front porch, she surrendered her to Sally and went upstairs. Mentally exhausted, Lolly hoped their evidence would be helpful to implicate the true guilty party. The three initials stayed on her mind, and as much as she tried, she couldn't connect them with anyone she knew in Coal Springs.

Before leaving home, Lolly took time to freshen up, style her hair, and dab lavender toilette water on her wrists and behind each ear. The lightweight summer dress she chose was comfortable and stylish. Lolly wanted to look nice for Ned. She made the final touches to her lip rouge in the mirror in the entry hall when her father walked in.

"You look nice. Where are you going?"

"I'm meeting Ned to discuss the trial."

"No, you're not. I will not allow it."

"You have no say so. Ned and Issac rode to Oden with me, and we all stayed in the Oden Hotel on the outskirts of town," she said, "If you paid attention to what's really important, you'd already know I've seen a lot of Ned lately."

"I demand you put a stop to it, or I will," he shouted.

"I'm over eighteen, and I don't listen to you anymore." Lolly opened the front door then stopped. "When you stop bringing whores into this house, then I'll stop seeing Ned." She slammed the door behind her and walked to the mercantile.

Lolly waited for Ned across the street from Crabtree's since the establishment was busy with the usual sorry crowd. Rowdy and intoxicated regulars filled the inside of the store while new farmhands lodging at the boarding house littered the outside. She tried to identify the newer ones. She didn't recognize any.

When she saw Ned walking in her direction, Lolly smoothed her dress and took a whiff of her wrist. The fragrance was still fresh.

"Hi, Ned," she said. "I'm waiting over here because of the sorry white trash over there."

"I don't blame you," he replied. "Do you have the tins?"

She handed him the satchel. "I transferred them into this when I got home."

"That's good. I'll throw it over my shoulder since it doesn't go with your pretty dress." He chuckled then added, "It'll look like I need supplies."

Lolly laughed, "Let's go."

ꟷ

When Ned and Lolly crossed the road, whistles and drunken insults were shouted at them.

"Whoa, boy, gettin' some tonight?" asked one.

"She's too pretty for you," said another. "Let me have her."

"You boys can't handle your liquor, much less a woman," Ned shot back.

They walked through the open door of the mercantile and looked for 'Ol Crabtree. More shouting and profanity commenced. A few of the prostitutes from the outskirts of the town accompanied the local men.

"Seen Crabtree?" Ned asked.

"He's in the back," said Joe Carne, a farmer from Eden.

Ned and Lolly scanned the shelf, stacked with chewing tobacco and cigarettes.

"Taken up, chawin'?" Joe asked.

"I tried some in Oden, and I wanted to see if Crabtree sold it," Ned answered.

"What's the brand?" Old man Foley asked.

"Bullshit or Bullwit, something like that," Ned answered.

"Bulwark," said Ol' Crabtree as he walked behind the counter. "I'm surprised, Ned. You don't look the type."

"What does the type look like?" Ned asked.

"A man that'd bring a gal like that into a place like this," Sam Pope uttered under his breath. "We know all about you two."

"Stifle it, Sam," said Crabtree. "Somebody like Joe or Ben," he said, and everyone laughed.

"In that case, maybe I shouldn't," said Ned. "Nah, do you have any Bulwark Cut Plug?"

As Crabtree glanced over the brands, Ned said, "That one in the white and green box."

"You're in luck, Ben usually wipes me out," Crabtree said.

Ned paid for the plug and took Lolly's arm. "See ya, boys." After crossing the road, he whispered, "That was easier than I thought."

Ned's thoughts remained on the names Crabtree mentioned. "Lolly, we need to find out Ben Smalley's full name."

"Why would Ben Smalley want to kill Rachel? What would be the motive?" Lolly asked. "Why would he be jealous of James?"

Ned remembered how Ben Smalley spoke to him about the murder charges against James and made crude comments about Lolly. However, he said nothing out of the ordinary during his testimony at the trial.

"Ben had to have a motive, but what could it have been?" Ned stopped. "The only connection they had was the boarding house. The answer lies there."

"Maybe we should pay the boarding house a visit," Lolly said.

~

Lolly pulled Ned's arm in the direction of the boarding house. It was located south of Coal Springs on the main road.

"We have to look the place over. If Smalley is there, we can get him to say something that might implicate him," said Lolly. "He's kind of simple anyway."

"I need to plan what I'm going to say. We can't hint about anything that might make Ben run."

It was dark, but they continued to walk. "There it is," said Lolly.

Horses and wagons were hitched to the front posts, while loud male voices and laughing women's loud laughter could be heard through the open front door. Two little girls played with a ball in the small side yard of the old house with no apparent supervision. A small sign hung on the gaslight post.

BOARDING - ROOMS AVAILABLE
$5 per week
Includes one Meal

"No wonder Rachel was so miserable," said Lolly. "This is a place for men, not women; especially not children."

A man ran out of the front door. "You better not set foot in this house again, you bastard," Ben Smalley shouted.

The man ran past Ned. "What's happened?"

"Smalley's crazy. His wife was all over me," the man said, out of breath. "He put his fist through the wall, then threw me out."

"Never mind, Ned," said Lolly. "I think I know his motive, but I need proof.

CHAPTER 23

FINDING THE TRUTH

"I think I know how to prove his motive," Lolly said as Ned opened the rusty gate at Serenity Farm and followed her into the property. "

"Good. When I devise the plan, it has to be in force starting tomorrow." Ned had to be certain about Smalley before they returned to Oden in two days.

"Look!" Lolly pointed to an upstairs window.

Ned felt in his pocket and grasped the watch pin. "It's probably Dandy."

The back door was ajar. Ned and Lolly walked into the kitchen to find the kettle cold and the floor unswept.

"This is how the house looked the first time I was here," Lolly said. She walked to the parlor and glanced toward the stairs. "There's a light burning."

They heard a loud noise from the upstairs hallway.

"What the hell?" Ned said.

Lolly grabbed Ned's arm as they walked in silence through the parlor, then climbed the stairs.

"Son-of-a-bitch," said a male voice. "Where are they?"

"That's Daddy!" Lolly whispered. "What's he doing here?"

"He's in my parent's bedroom," he said as they heard knocking and kicking sounds.

Lolly stood in the doorway and said, "Daddy? Why are you here?"

Dr. Hanes jumped with a start. "I could ask you the same," Dr. Hanes answered. "I own this place. I can be in this house or on the property anytime I please."

"We saw the light from the road. There should be no lights in this house," Lolly answered, then noticed her father's clothing was smeared with dust and plaster.

"What are you looking for, sir?" Ned asked.

"Ned, you'll be glad to hear the developers in Birmingham have withdrawn the offer for the property," the doctor said as he brushed the dusty powder from his pants. "It seems they paid a visit to Serenity Farm while we were in Oden, and claim the entire property is haunted or possessed."

Ned looked at Lolly, "In what way? Did they elaborate?"

"No, and it doesn't matter." Dr. Hanes backed away from the wall he'd broken a hole through. "Son, you can have this place, and I'm glad to be rid of it. And by the way, the Birmingham people reported rats or other kinds of vermin scurrying through the walls. That's what I was looking for."

Ned plopped down on the dusty floor. "I can't believe it. What form of payment do you need?"

"We'll sort all that out. I tried to get all I could for this place. You win, you're meant to live here with the haints," the doctor said. "I'll have the transfer of the deed drawn up."

Lolly ran to her father. "Daddy, I knew you'd come to your senses."

"What you said before you left the house opened my eyes to my recent behavior." Dr. Hanes said. "I haven't been an ideal father."

"No, you haven't." Lolly began. "Ned is a good person, and you've done nothing but humiliate him concerning this property."

Dr. Hanes looked at Ned. "It helped put your defenses up, fight for what is yours, and you're all the stronger for it."

"What do you mean?" Lolly had a confused look on her face. "And why did you buy the place anyway?"

"One day, I'll tell you both." Dr. Hanes headed to the stairs. "It doesn't matter anymore."

After Dr. Hanes left the property, Ned asked, "What did he mean by that? I have to know the reason he forced my parents out."

"Right now, we need to concentrate on Rachel and how we're going to prove it was Smalley." Lolly looked around at the mess her father made in the bedroom.

"This bedroom is empty, didn't you notice?" Ned asked. "Rachel must not be here."

Ned reminded her about the first time she came into the house, and how the condition was the same as now. Ned realized the garden and the house were brought to life only when Dandy and Rachel were there.

"They usually don't reveal themselves when strange or undesirable visitors enter the gate, but I guess they did when the Birmingham people came."

"So, Dandy must be a spirit, too," she said.

"It seems so," Ned answered. "It all makes sense now."

Ned stood up and checked the secret compartment. Finding the velvet box, he opened it to a note which read:

My love is home again, and your despair will be gone.

Stay with me and keep my heart. I will never fade away.

Your path of truth has almost reached the end. Only one step to go.

I send much love to you both, and I will see you again.

"What is meant by 'one step to go?'" Lolly glanced around the room. "She's here; I feel it."

All at once Ned saw a flash in the corner of the room. "Rachel?" A vapor formed in the corner, revealing a woman. "Rachel?" Ned asked again.

This woman was older, with dark hair and eyes. She also wore a flowing white gown and carried a red rose.

"Mother," Ned whispered, "it's you."

"Yes, Ned. I'm with you every day. The answer you seek is closer than you think. Take the last step," Leona said as she began to fade.

"Mother, wait!"

All Lolly could say was, "She's so lovely. There must be something she wants you to know."

"That must be the last answer," he said. But what answer was closer than he thought? "Lolly, where do you look for answers?"

"In my daddy's files, but I can't find the key. He changed the hiding place," she said.

"I know where it is, he showed me a month or so ago," said Ned. "Are the files where you'll find Smalley's motive?"

"I think we can count on it. I wonder why Daddy showed you?" Lolly started down the stairs. It was dark, but she knew which steps to avoid.

"He said he had a reason for showing me where the keys and the files were," Ned said. "I don't know why. Maybe we'll find out."

When they opened the gate, Ned remarked, "Lolly, thank you for everything. If you hadn't gone to the creek without me that day, we would have no evidence, nothing."

"I loved Rachel. She was my best friend," she said. "Nothing could have kept me away."

Lolly waited for Ned on the front porch. It was early morning, and Dr. Hanes left to make a house call in Riverton. She hoped Ned would come on since her daddy could be back soon.

Ned rode up on General Lee and attached him to the hitching post.

"Hurry!" she shouted. "Daddy took the carriage to Riverton and could be home before lunch."

Ned led Lolly down the long hall to Dr. Hanes's library. He stopped at the massive ornate bookcase and retrieved the large keyring from the drawer. "I'm not sure which one opens the door," he said.

"It's this one." Lolly picked out a large metal key. She opened the heavy door and walked toward the desk. "This is for the file cabinet." A smaller key unlocked the wooden drawers and revealed years of files for almost every member of the small community.

"Where should I look first?" Lolly asked.

"How about Smalley and his wife? That should be interesting."

Lolly skimmed through the patients whose name began with S. After finding Theodore Benjamin Smalley's; she handed the file to Ned.

"Hmm, T. S. B. Three months ago, he weighed one hundred ninety-five pounds. That's a big man," he said as he continued to look. "He suffers from gout, has a lung condition, and has been sterile since 1902." Ned looked at Lolly. "Those little girls aren't his."

"Maybe they're from his wife's first marriage," Lolly suggested.

"No, they were married when the younger girls were born. I remember my father was happy for Ben." I guess no one knew he was infertile. Look for Vera's now."

Lolly found Vera Smalley's file behind Ben's. "I'll look at this one," she said as she opened it.

"Don't hold anything back just because she's a woman," said Ned.

"Okay, she is thirty-nine years old and has borne three children," Lolly read. "The first 1890, the second in 1902, and the third in 1904. All girls."

Ned noticed Lolly's mouth drop. "What is it?"

"I can't believe it," she began, "The father of the baby girl in 1890 was Noble Clair."

"What?" Ned ripped the file out of her hand. "Is Vera Smalley Rachel's actual mother?"

"It seems so. What about the younger girls?" Lolly asked.

"Vera got around, it seems," said Ned. "The second girl's father is a name I don't recognize."

"And the youngest?"

Ned skimmed down to the last baby's record. "Who do you think it is? Take a wild guess."

"James Cason," she said. "I'm not a bit surprised." She thought a moment. "But he wasn't in town in 1904, was he?"

"He's worked fall harvest around here since 1903," said Ned. "I remember seeing him in town, but never met him."

"My father's files hold a multitude of sins and secrets," said Lolly. "We'd better quit before he comes home."

"Wait. Look for Foley's file," Ned couldn't wait to hear this. "His should be a shocker, too."

Lolly found Foley. "He had typhoid fever in 1900, which left him with gastrointestinal problems. He also suffers from syphilis and genital herpes." She looked up and said, "That man is disgusting. I'll check his wife's file, too." She pulled out Agnes Foley's file. "She has no signs of any of those afflictions. But she gave birth to an illegitimate daughter in 1888. I guess being free of any syphilis and herpes means she and her husband have never done the dirty deed. It's a sin, you know."

As Lolly placed the file back in its rightful place, they heard a carriage pull to the back of the house. "That's Daddy," she said.

They returned all the files and secured the cabinet. Making sure nothing was out of place, Ned and Lolly left the library, locked the door, and placed the keyring back into the large drawer.

"I always wondered why Rachel always called her mother Ada," Lolly said. "Do you think she knew the truth?"

CHAPTER 24

JUSTICE

After taking their seats with the spectators in the courtroom, Ned held tight to the tobacco tins, while Lolly and Issac glanced around the room for Ben Smalley.

Sam Hastings entered the room and took his seat at the defense table. Ned needed to inform him of the findings.

"Do I just go up to him?"

"Yes, go now before the judge comes in," whispered Lolly.

"Mr. Hastings, I have the evidence needed to free James Cason," Ned said.

"Sit down," Hastings said.

Ned proceeded to explain the tobacco tins and the connection of the brand to Smalley.

"We should be able to use the information about the tins, but we need a reliable source to back it up. Hastings said.

"Foley can back it up," said Ned.

"Okay, I'll call Foley back to the stand if I need to. I'll start by calling Smalley first," Hastings said. "But I'll need the tins in my possession as physical evidence."

"There are other reasons I can't divulge that would cause Ben Smalley to hold a grudge against Cason. Please trust me on that," Ned began. "The tobacco tins should be enough evidence to charge him."

With reluctance, Ned gave the tins to Sam Hastings. He hoped the lawyer had enough gumption to rile the man into a confession.

"All rise."

Judge Greene took his place and brought the court to order. "Mr. Comer, call your first witness."

"The prosecution rests, Your Honor," Comer said.

Sam Hastings stood. "I'd like to call Ben Smalley to the stand."

Lolly grabbed Ned's arm. "I think he's considered a hostile witness. I'm not sure, though."

With a confused look, Ben walked to the front of the courtroom. The bailiff reminded him he was still under oath.

"Mr. Smalley, are you a smoking or chawing man?" Hastings asked as he walked around the defense table.

"Sometimes."

"When you smoke, is it at home or elsewhere?"

"My wife doesn't like to smell the smoke or have spittoons in the house, so I usually go outside," he said.

"Where do you go? Out in the road, your back porch, while you're taking a walk?"

"All of those places, I guess," he said.

"What brand do you chaw?" Hastings asked.

"I'm partial to Bulwark Plug." He wiped his forehead with his handkerchief.

"Is this what the tin box looks like?" Hastings held up the rusty tobacco tin Ned had given him.

"That looks like one," Ben Smalley said.

"How do most people store plugs, snuff, or cigarettes, Mr. Smalley?" he asked. "And I'm referring to men and women."

Smalley looked confused and irritated but continued to answer the question. "Some use tin boxes, fancy metal boxes, and other ways, I guess."

"How do you store your snuff?"

"Different ways. I use a tin box most of the time. That's all I have now." Ben's voice rose, indicating frustration. "What does this have to do with anything?"

"I'm asking the questions, sir," said Hastings. "What other types of containers you use?"

"I used to have an old silver box with my father's initials engraved on the top," he began, "my father passed it down to me a long time ago."

"What happened to it?"

"I lost it somewhere; I don't' know."

"If you were to smoke a cigarette, what brand would you choose, Mr. Smalley?"

Ned could see Ben Smalley squirm in the witness chair. The man was either mad or knew where the questioning was going.

"My cigarette of choice is Chesterfield."

"Thank you, Mr. Smalley," Hastings said. "Please excuse me for a moment."

Sam Hastings walked to the defense table, opened his leather pouch, and retrieved one item.

Lolly gripped Ned's arm, then glanced over at Issac. Ned sat on the edge of his seat.

"Mr. Smalley, do you hold a serious grudge against James Cason?" Hastings asked as he stood next to the defense table.

"No, why should I?"

"Mr. Smalley, do you recognize this item?" Sam Hastings held up the silver cigarette case engraved with the worn off initials T. S. B.

"I'm not sure," he said. "I'd have to look at it a little closer."

"Be my guest." Hastings approached the witness stand and handed over the silver box.

Ben Smalley took the silver box and examined it. He opened it to find a piece of paper inside that read, *"You're caught."* Ben looked up at the lawyer and jumped up from the witness chair. He attempted to jump over the short railing to make a quick escape.

"I wouldn't do that, Mr. Smalley. You can't get too far since I expected as much from you. Our deputies are standing by."

"Sit down, Mr. Smalley," Judge Greene shouted.

Ned tried to stay calm but gave Lolly a quick hug and shook Issac's hand. The spectators on the floor and in the gallery erupted in surprised excitement. Even James Cason looked up and forced a smile.

"I'll clear this court again!" shouted the judge.

The courtroom was silent as Sam Hastings continued to question Smalley. "Why did you beat Rachel Clair Cason to death?"

"I don't know."

"What do you mean, you don't know." Hastings raised his voice. "What was your motive?"

"I don't know."

Hastings was irritated. "Again, Mr. Smalley, do you hold a grudge against James Cason?"

"Yes."

"What is that grudge?"

"I can't say."

"Mr. Smalley, it's clear you murdered Rachel Clair Cason. You can say."

Ben Smalley remained silent.

"Answer my question, Ben Smalley!" Hastings shouted in Smalley's face and slammed his fist on the railing.

"Because he was screwing my wife!" Ben Smalley placed his head in his hands.

"Why didn't you just kill Cason? Why did you murder an innocent young mother?"

"Because I wanted them both to suffer."

"Both?"

"My wife Vera, and Cason."

"What? Where did Rachel Cason come in? What was her connection, besides being married to Cason? She was the one to suffer the most."

"Because Vera was Rachel Clair's natural mother, and she worried about her. Noble Clair had an affair with Vera in 1890, which produced Rachel. Vera was married to me, and I refused to take the child into my house. And because my wife is nothing but a whore."

"Mr. Smalley, what is James Cason's connection to all this, besides the affair with your wife?"

"Vera's youngest daughter is James Cason's. Their affair has been going on for years. It began when he was around seventeen," Smalley began to sob. "He comes back every fall, and they take up where they left off."

"Why murder the girl so brutally? She was innocent."

"After all these years, I wanted to hurt them both. I chose Rachel. When I hit her the first time, my rage consumed me. I was blind to who I was beating. All I could see was Vera's face before me." Ben Smalley lowered his head.

The courtroom was silent, and Sam Hastings continued to stand in front of the witness stand. "Your Honor, I charge this person, Ben Smalley, with the murder of Rachel Clair Cason, and I ask for dismissal of murder charges against the defendant, James Cason."

Judge Greene pounded the gavel and said, "All murder charges against James Cason are now dismissed. The court is adjourned."

Two deputies held Ben Smalley as one more placed handcuffs on his wrists. They led him out the side door of the courtroom.

Tears streamed down Lolly's face. "It's over."

"It's all because of you, Lolly," said Ned. "All because you went to Cain Creek early that day. If it hadn't been the exact time for the sun to shine on that spot, you never would've seen the glare on the silver box."

"It was the both of ya," said Issac. "Y'all makes a good team."

Ned and James exchanged glances before they left. He was going back to jail, but not for this crime. James nodded a thank you.

"Let's go home, boys," said Lolly.

~

"I'm mighty proud of you two," Dr. Hanes said. "How did you figure it all out?"

"We'll tell you the details someday, but it was love for Rachel and determination," said Ned. "Lolly was the primary investigator, though. I give her most of the credit."

"What are your plans for Serenity Farm, now that you're the owner of the deed?" the doctor asked.

"The harvest is the top priority. I plan to ask Issac to stay on at the Clair farm," Ned answered, "but Ada still owns it."

"Ada should be coming home very soon. She's making great strides with her progress," said the doctor.

Ned noticed how quiet Lolly seemed. "What's the matter?"

"Oh, nothing, I guess. Now that our investigation is over, I'm afraid we'll rarely see each other, what with Serenity Farm and all," she said. "And I'm thinking about how much I'll miss Josie when she goes back to her grandmother."

~

Ada Clair came back to her farm in October. She was glad to be home but felt it would be too hard to live alone in the house. As she looked around the farm, tears filled her eyes.

"How does it feel to be back home?" Dr. Hanes asked.

"Justus, there are so many memories here, and I can't take care of this place alone, especially with Ned moving back to Serenity Farm."

"I think we can work out something. What do you think, Lolly?" Dr. Hanes said.

"Mrs. Clair, you're welcome to stay with us until other plans can be made," said Lolly. "I know Josie will be so happy to have you home."

"You're so kind. I've missed her."

Ned approached with a grin and tipped his worn hat. "Ada, Issac has agreed to stay on here and tend to the farm." He glanced at Lolly and smiled.

Ada smiled and swiped at a tear. "Ned, please tell him how glad I am to hear it."

"Tell him yourself. Here he comes." Ned waved him over.

"Ma'am, Miss Lolly," Issac greeted. "I welcomes ya home."

"Issac, I've been told you're staying to tend my farm, and I'm happy about it," Ada began. "Since you'll be in charge, I think you should bring your family here and live in the main house."

Issac removed his hat and covered his eyes with his hand. After a moment, he raised his head, and tears streamed down his face. "Mrs. Clair, Ma'am, I'd be so proud ta do jus that, an I thanks ya."

"Where is your family?" Ned asked. "Close-by, I hope."

"Yas, they stays in Riverton. My wife, Kiz, an two big strappin' boys. They be old enough ta helps on the farm."

"Do you know where Martha is, Justus?" Ada asked. "Don't you think it's time she came home?"

"Ada, you know those circumstances. Martha left Lolly and me when our girls were about five months old," he said. "Don't you remember how you, Noble, and I committed to never speak of our situations again and to go on with our lives?"

"Oh, yes," she said. "But being in the hospital taught me to tell the truth and not let hypocrisy dictate our lives," she began, "the so-called 'pillars of the community,' including you, ruined my family. Don't you think it's time to tell Lolly the truth?"

"I will, one day. Not now."

Lolly came into the parlor with Josie. The baby reached for her grandmother. "What are you all talking about?" she asked.

"About telling the truth," Ada said as she looked at Dr. Hanes. "Don't you have something to tell Lolly, Justus?"

Dr. Hanes looked at Ada Clair with a furrowed brow. "I'll tell her later."

"Tell me what? I want to know if it concerns me," Lolly demanded.

"Justus, tell this girl who her mother is," Ada shouted. "Do it or I will."

"Daddy? What is she talking about?"

Dr. Hanes let out a deep breath and stood up. He walked over to Lolly and took her hand. "Follow me."

The doctor led his daughter down the long hall to his library. He took the keyring out of the drawer and unlocked the heavy door. He unlocked the file cabinet and opened it. "Are you sure you want to know?"

"Yes, Daddy, but I'm confused. My real mother? I thought my mother left us when I was a baby," Lolly said.

Dr. Hanes looked through the files until he found the one he was looking for. He hesitated before pulling it out. He sat down on the red velvet settee and motioned for her to sit by him.

"I want you to listen to me when I tell you this." The doctor took a deep breath. "I loved your natural mother with all my heart, but she wasn't free. She was married and had an older child," he said. "I know it was wrong, but I continue to think about her almost daily."

"Wasn't Martha my natural mother?" Lolly asked.

"I married Martha in 1888. We loved each other when we married, but soon, she was unhappy and wanted me to move to a large city and build my medical practice."

"Why didn't you?"

"Coal Springs is my home. I was raised here and didn't want to leave."

"I'm confused. If Martha isn't my real mother, then who is?"

He opened the file of Leona McClure. On May 24, 1890, she delivered a baby girl. Name of father-Dr. Justus Landry Hanes.

"This means Ned McClure is your brother," he said. "I know how you feel about him."

Lolly was stunned. She sat on the red settee and said nothing.

"I don't know what to say, except we've done pretty well for ourselves, haven't we, you and I?" the doctor asked.

"No wonder Martha left us," Lolly shouted. "You'd better tell Ned why you drove his parents out of town!" She ran out of the room sobbing.

Dr. Hanes put his head in his hands and asked, "What have I done?"

Lolly drove the Roadster to the Clair farm. She had based her entire future on Ned. Now everything had changed. He was her brother, for heaven sakes. You can't love a brother like that. She pulled into the Clair farm and saw Ned and Issac. Blowing the horn, she got their attention.

"Ned, I need to talk to you." Lolly created a dust storm with the brakes.

What's the matter?"

"You'd better sit down," she said. "Martha Hanes is not my real mother."

"Huh? What do you mean?" Ned sat on the back of the buckboard.

"Daddy showed me my natural mother's medical file from the day I was born in 1890." She was out of breath. "The file he showed me was Leona McClure's."

He looked at Lolly with a question. "Do you mean your father was 'L'?" Ned asked. "I knew my mother had someone's baby, and it wasn't my father's."

"How did you know?" Lolly asked.

"The first time I went back to Serenity Farm, I found a note tucked inside the velvet box of the secret compartment. It said something about 'our baby' and how he couldn't stand for my father to touch her," he said through gritted teeth. "He signed it 'L.'"

"His full name is Justus Landry Hanes." Then Lolly smiled. "It seems you're my brother. This must be our last step on the path of truth."

"Does anyone call him Landry?" Ned asked.

"My grandmother did, and your mother, it seems." Lolly suddenly felt relieved. "So, I guess you know why my father drove your parents out of town."

"No, there has to be more to it than that," he said.

"What are you going to do?"

"Let's go," Ned said. "We need more answers from the doctor."

Ned and Lolly found the doctor sitting with his head in his hands at his desk in the library. "Dr. Hanes, we need answers," said Ned.

"I've said all I want to say."

"No, Daddy. There has to be much more," Lolly said. "You can't break this news to us then stop talking."

"Why did you foreclose on my parents and shame us out of town?" Ned asked with clenched fists. "Was it to save your face? Was it to ruin our lives?"

"No, I don't know," the doctor replied.

"Yes, you do know," Ned shouted. "You killed my mother with shame and disgrace." Ned paced the floor, running his hands through his hair. "Why did you do it?"

"I loved Leona with all my heart. Never did I want to hurt her," he said. "Your father found out about us soon before Lolly was born." The doctor wiped his perspiring forehead. "He challenged me to a duel. He didn't care if dueling was illegal in the state; he wanted one of us dead." Dr. Hanes stood and faced Ned. "I declined."

"What about Leona?" Lolly asked. "Didn't she have anything to say about the situation?"

"Josiah decided Leona's punishment would be to give you up." Dr. Hanes walked to the portrait of Martha Hanes and stopped. "Josiah McClure told Martha all the sordid details. We'd wanted a child eventually, so she gave in and agreed to take you."

"When did the affair start?" Ned asked. "I was two years old at the time of Lolly's birth."

"I loved Leona since we were children. She said she'd wait for me. I went off to college, then medical school, and then wasn't sure if I'd ever return to Coal Springs," he began. "There were so many opportunities in larger cities." He lit a cigar and returned to his desk.

"But you came back, Daddy. Why?"

"I couldn't bear to live without Leona. When I finished medical school and came home, she had married a transient farmhand, Josiah, and Ned was a baby. I'd been away for seven years."

"You still didn't answer my question about the foreclosure," said Ned.

"I wanted to hurt them both. Leona refused to see me again," he began. "She loved Josiah and said I'd been away too long. She finally agreed to see me. We talked, and one thing led to another," he said as he took a pull from the cigar.

"So, you waited years for an excuse and used his illness to humiliate them," said Ned. "Then, when I came back, you humiliated me in every way you could."

"That about sums it up," the doctor said. "I wanted to make you fight for the farm. Look, let's put all this behind us."

"That's impossible," said Ned as he walked out of the room.

"I will be packing my things as soon as Ada is settled in a home of her own," said Lolly. "I needed a mother. Why didn't you try to work things out with Martha?"

"I married her on the rebound. I thought I loved her," the doctor said. "She didn't want to raise another woman's child."

"No, that's not it. I understand Martha now," Lolly said. "She and I are alike; it seems. Martha didn't want to be anywhere near the likes of you."

൭൬

As Ned walked back to the Clair farm, his thoughts were on nothing but how much he missed his parents. Josiah McClure was a man worth a thousand Justus Hanes'. Now he knew the truth, and it hurt.

"Ned," Lolly shouted. "Wait."

He turned as Lolly approached. "You know I've had feelings for you since our days at Coal Springs School," she said.

"I know. I could tell," said Ned. "I knew there was a reason I couldn't return those feelings. And it wasn't Rachel."

"You and I do have a kind of relationship. We formed a special bond with each other. After all, we've been through a lot together," Lolly said as she took his hand. "I know the feeling I have isn't the kind of love you had with Rachel, but a different sort."

"Do you love me like a brother?"

Lolly laughed. "Yes, that kind of love."

Ned smiled, "I always wanted a sister, and I'm glad it's you."

EPILOGUE

MARCH 1995

"Miss Montgomery, are you finished with the files you took home with you on Friday?" It was Mr. Meeks. "If you are, would you mind dropping them off at the office sometime today?"

"Yes, sir. I'll be glad to." I wasn't finished, but I had to turn them over to him.

I dropped off the files and my boring Sunday afternoon turned into a drive to Oden County to find Coal Springs. After reading the old articles from the archives, I had to go there. My obsession had taken over.

The county was close enough to take a day trip, and maybe I'd find more information about the town and my heritage. I packed lunch and filled a Thermos. I drove out of the city to lose myself in the country where living is simple, and the lush scenery remains intact.

Old State Highway 78 is a beautiful, scenic byway that connects Birmingham to points east and past Atlanta. The day was warm, and the azaleas were in full bloom. Dogwood trees in white and pink lined the highway, and the clear blue sky could be seen through the branches of the old trees. Farms are still abundant outside of the city, and cows sprinkle the hillsides at the base of the Appalachian Mountains.

Soon, I noticed a small highway sign with an arrow that read:

Coal Springs
Home of Natural Sparkling Waters

I found it. Coal Springs was only five miles off the highway, so I turned left.

The county route had no number. I shrugged and pressed on. The springtime splendor was lush on this country road. Trails for tractors seemed plentiful, but I didn't see any modern farm equipment anywhere. The air smelled of wisteria and privet. The purple grape shaped blooms of the wisteria vines had overtaken the small, spindly trees and split rail fences on the side of the road. The enigma of it all was breathtaking.

After driving the five miles, I approached a historical marker.

SITE OF THE
MOUNTAIN LODGE HOTEL
1890-1952

I stopped the car and looked around. There was nothing but an old abandoned building with a partial veranda and a tall railroad trestle. I walked closer and found what was left of two grass tennis courts and a swimming pool. A crumbling open-air building stood close to a few decaying cabins from a long time gone. A faded sign hung on the side of the open-air building that read, *The Pavilion.* It must have been the center for all the social activity.

Disappointed, I returned to the car and started back to Highway 78. I saw a farmer and his wife approaching and stopped to ask for information.

"I'm looking for the community of Coal Springs. Which way do I turn?"

"Yes, ma'am," he said. "Go through the railroad tunnel ahead, then turn left. There isn't much left of the old town."

"Thank you."

After I drove through the old tunnel, the paved road came to an end, and a dirt road forked to the right and left. I took a left and saw the tall trestle in the distance. The road was fair, but a bit bumpy for my car. The scenery was beautiful beyond description. There were hills and steep ridges, a picturesque creek, and some of the most massive trees I'd ever seen. The dirt road ended, so I parked and got out. An old abandoned train track, camouflaged by years of overgrowth and neglect, peeked out from a mass of wisteria vines. The breeze carried the wisteria scent, so I grabbed my lunch and Thermos and started to explore. I came to a thick row of old magnolia trees that were so large, the branches reminded me of octopus tendrils, as they rested on the ground. I couldn't see through them, but I found a small path which led to the other side. Coal Springs must be close-by.

Suddenly, the wind picked up, and I was forced to hold tight to one of the tree branches. The strong wind blew some of the large leaves off the trees, and I closed my eyes and shielded my face from flying debris. When the gale-force wind calmed, I could barely see a small community on the other side of the magnolias. A few old buildings were lining a dirt road. I heard a distant train whistle, and the haunting sound of it caused me to feel as if I'd traveled back in time.

"Ma'am, are you okay?" A young girl, about six years old stood on the other side of the row of magnolias.

"Yes, I guess so." I heard voices from behind the trees. "I'm looking for Coal Springs. Is it close-by?"

"It's this way," she said. "You can come with me if you want to."

"Sure, thank you." I continued to hold my brown lunch bag and Thermos. My long hair was a mess from the strong wind, and my brush was in my purse, which I left in the car.

The young girl wore a thin gingham dress with a large white collar, thick tights, and ankle boots. *That's a strange outfit.* A large matching bow sat on the crown of her head. I noticed the child looking at my white t-shirt and jeans.

"What's your name," she asked. "Mine's Josie Hanes."

"My name is Rachel, and I'm from Birmingham."

I followed Josie to the dirt road and noticed an old general store with older men sitting out front. I looked down the main street where horses and wagons were hitched to posts, and antique cars were parked in front of old houses.

"I'll stop following you now Josie. Thank you for showing me the way."

"Don't you want to come and meet my mama? We live right down here," she said. Josie's hair was blonde like mine.

"Okay." We passed a stately old house with a large front porch and a doctor's Rod of Asclepius symbol on a sign hanging from a post. I continued to follow her until she stopped at a rusty fence. Inside was the most beautiful farmhouse and gardens I'd ever seen. Josie opened the squeaky old gate and proceeded to show off her mama's herb garden.

"My mama loves to grow herbs. She puts them in our food."

Pink, purple, and white azaleas were covered in large blooms, and red tulips grew in a sunny row that bordered the small front porch. I noticed a sign hanging on the railing. "Serenity Farm."

"Mama, I have a new friend," Josie called through the back door. "She's from Birmingham."

A very attractive young woman opened the back door and said, "Josie, I've been looking all over for…."

"Mama, this is Rachel; I don't know her last name yet," she said. "My mama's name is Lolly Hanes."

"I'm glad to meet you, Lolly. Josie was so kind as to lead me here. My left my car on the other side of the magnolia trees near that general store," I said, noticing her odd expression and old-fashioned style of dress. "Your gardens are lovely, and I've never seen azaleas so beautiful."

"Josie, go find your Uncle Ned, please," Lolly said. "Come in, Rachel."

I followed the young woman into the small kitchen. There were an authentic country wood stove and a deep porcelain sink with a water pump attached to the side. The aroma of hickory and spices filled the room. This house was old but looked almost new.

With a shaky voice, Lolly asked, "Would you like something to drink?"

"Thank you, no," I said. "I brought a sack lunch and a Thermos of cold water." I unscrewed the top of the Thermos and poured the water into the companion cup.

"I've never seen such a thing," Lolly said. "Did you get that in Birmingham?"

"Yes, I did," I answered. The back door opened to Josie running in and sitting next to me.

"Uncle Ned's coming," she said. "Rachel, what's your last name?"

"Montgomery, like the capital," I said.

The back door swung open again. "Ned, I'd like you to meet Rachel Montgomery," Lolly said. "Josie's new friend."

Standing before me was the most handsome man I'd ever seen. His worn shirt and dirty dungarees offset the dark hair and blue eyes. His hair was a mess, and I couldn't speak. Neither could he because his intense blue eyes fixed on mine, and I found it hard to hear his voice.

"I'm pleased to meet you, Rachel," he said with his hand out.

I shook his hand. He was a farmer, but his hands were soft and warm. I couldn't stop looking at him.

"Let me show you around," he said.

Ned led me into the parlor and dining room. "The restoration is perfect," I said.

"Yes, it took my sister and me about two years to finish." He looked puzzled. "How did you know it's a restoration?"

"It has to be. This house looks to be from the late 1800s. A building dating back one-hundred years would need major renovation. I'm familiar with old homes and buildings from that era. I work closely with an architect, and my firm specializes in the old, historic areas of Birmingham to renovate."

"You're an architect? I thought that was a man's profession," he said. "One-hundred years ago?"

Before I could answer, he led me to a staircase railing detailed with some of the most exquisite artisan carvings I'd seen.

"I don't need to see the upstairs. I must be going anyway." I looked at my watch. It was only three o'clock. I felt uneasy. As we walked back to the kitchen, I passed a grouping of old photographs on the piano. I look at Ned, then back to the picture. "That photo looks like one I've seen recently." It was the photograph of the two little girls and the woman with the baby. The paper wasn't yellowed and worn.

"Rachel, I've been keeping the watch brooch in my pocket since Dandy gave it to me." Ned removed something from his pocket. "He told me if I had it, you would visit, and I've waited a long time."

He handed me the watch brooch, and I examined it closely. The antique piece of jewelry had the year 1890 engraved on the back, but it didn't look one-hundred years old. "I don't know anyone named Dandy." I was frightened. *Think, does any of this seem familiar? Ned McClure. Does that name mean anything to me?*

Ned walked me out the front door and into the beautiful garden. "This garden almost flooded from the heavy rainstorms we had last month," he said. "Then the late snow and ice storms killed a lot of the new growth on the azaleas and dogwoods. Look at them now."

"What do you mean? They're beautiful." I also noticed how the abundant cotton field stretched as far as the eye could see.

"They weren't yesterday," Ned said. "I knew you were coming to visit when I saw how the gardens looked this morning." He waved at a black gentleman and his wife driving a horse and wagon on the dusty main road. "Afternoon, Issac, Miss Kiz."

"Will you take me back to my car?" *Was this man crazy?* "I need to get back."

"Of course, I'll tell Lolly."

"Miss Kiz?" I said out loud. The woman on the wagon was fortyish with thick glasses. When Ned returned, I asked, "Did you ever know an Annie Smalley?"

"She's a child that used to live at the boarding house with her sister and mother. They left town soon after their father was sent to jail," he said. "Why do you ask?"

"I read the name somewhere. I was curious." I felt shaky. Something was happening to me. *Was I dreaming?*

"Ready to go?" Ned asked.

"Yes, but I'd like to walk through town if I could. I need a pack of gum, and I saw a store down the street."

When we left, Lolly and Josie waved from the front porch. "Please come back soon," they shouted. Lolly dabbed tears from her eyes.

We walked to the old mercantile store. "Why does the store look so familiar?" I said. "I must have seen a picture of it in a magazine."

"It used to be Crabtree's Mercantile, but he died, and a Mr. Cooper bought the store," he said. "Do you want to go in?"

"No, I changed my mind," I said. "What's straight ahead on this road?"

"Nothing much. The old boarding house used to be in that clearing to the right, but it was destroyed by fire a year ago," he said. "Sadly, three people died in the fire. No one wanted to rebuild so the lot remains empty."

"Driving in, I saw a beautiful creek. Is a part of it close-by?" I asked.

"You must mean Cain Creek. The most beautiful part is about ten minutes away."

"Would you mind taking me?" I suddenly felt safe with Ned. "Is this Mennonite country?

"No. That's an odd question," Ned said as we walked down the tree-lined main street. "Why would you ask that?"

"The farm wagons and the old-fashioned style of dress," I answered. "I haven't seen any modern farm equipment."

"What we have is as modern as you can get," he said as he looked at my clothes. "You're wearing tight men's dungarees. What kind of attire is that?"

We soon stopped at a branch with a tiny string tied to it. We turned in and followed a well-worn path which led to a clearing. Suddenly I felt cold and was filled with fear. "I need to go." I ran to the road.

"Rachel, stop," Ned shouted. "Do you remember anything?"

"Something scared me while I stood by the water. I don't know what."

He placed his arm around me, and we walked back through the beautiful old town. We found the path through the row of magnolia trees and looked for my car.

"Where's my car? I parked it by an old railroad track. It was overgrown with weeds and vines."

"Let's look over this way." Ned led me to a railroad track that looked fully functional. No weeds or vines were hiding the rails, and the tall trestle could be seen in the distance. "Do you see your car?"

"No. Where is it? What's happening to me?" I felt sick and more frightened. "What year is this?"

Ned looked at me and smiled. "Today is March 14, 1913."

I looked at Ned and had the strange impulse to ask, "Who was the murdered girl found floating in Cain Creek in 1909?"

"Do you believe in miracles?" Ned asked.

"You didn't answer my question, Ned."

"Her name was Rachel Clair, and I'm looking at her now."

"What do you mean? I'm frightened, and I want to go home."

"Don't be. You're finally home, Rachel. Your home is with me."

"This isn't my home. I've never been here in my life," I shouted and ran away from him. "This is a dream."

He called out to me, "Think. Isn't it all familiar? Don't you remember me?"

This entire experience was a nightmare. Ned followed close behind and shouted for me to stop. I continued to run through the trees and back into the beautiful old town. I stopped at the rusty gate of Serenity Farm. I do remember growing up in this town. I remember Lolly, my parents, and Ned as well as James Cason and Ben Smalley. I also remember Serenity Farm and how the beauty of it took me away from the scrutiny, and wickedness of the community. Ned caught up, and before we opened the gate, I asked, "What happened to the church?"

He smiled. "The sins of the devout" became well known, and most of them left the area. I hear the few that didn't leave continue to meet at Widow Crabtree's house for Bible study, and Dr. Hanes lives all alone in that great big house. The Coal Springs Church folded and is now an empty building." He put his arms around me. "Lolly is my sister and Josie is…."

"My daughter." I tried to hold back the tears. "How do I explain my growing up in Birmingham? Was I reincarnated?" Then the inevitable question. "Have I traveled back in time?"

"Let's just say coming back to us is a miracle," Ned began, "and there is never an explanation for a miracle."

I was in a state of shock, but when I said the words, "let's go home," a feeling of peace and serenity washed over me. I was where I belonged.

Lolly, Ada Clair, and Josie walked out of the screen door and stood on the porch. "Welcome home, Rachel," Ada said. "We've missed you so."

"Mother." I looked at Ned and said, "I remember it all now." I brought his hand to my cheek and looked into his blue eyes. "Yes, I'm home, and I will never leave you again."

"Hello, Mr. Meeks. This is Joe Neely, the lead detective on the Rachel Montgomery case. Please give me a call. We have located Miss Montgomery's car. You have my number."

Tom Meeks quickly returned the call.

"Miss Montgomery's car was found about five miles off Highway 78 near the former location of Coal Springs in Oden County," Neely said.

"Are you positive it was her car?"

"Yes, sir. Her purse was still inside. Does she have any family members we can call to report our findings?"

"No, she had no family."

Mr. Meeks was filled with sadness as he reached for the folders Rachel Montgomery dropped off before she disappeared. He opened one that held an assortment of old photographs. As he sifted through them, one fell to the floor. It was a hand-tinted postcard with the photograph of a lovely young blonde woman, a child, and an infant. "That's Rachel Montgomery. No, it can't be," he said. Mr. Meeks read the caption at the bottom. *Mrs. Rachel McClure, daughter Josephine, and Ned Jr. 1915.* There was one more postcard, also hand-tinted. This one was a wedding picture, and the caption read *Mr. and Mrs. Ned McClure on their wedding day 1914.*

Tom Meeks spent the day at his desk going through the stack of folders Rachel had diligently collected for his restorations. He wanted to find more photographs of the young blonde woman to confirm the unthinkable.

The last folder wasn't as thick as the others and contained information on the buildings of the five points area of Southside in 1887, then called the Town of Highland. This area was one of the first suburbs of Birmingham and rich in the opulent architecture of the era. Meeks found a few later images of the grand homes and the area, but one made him stop and push the others aside.

The black and white image was a close-up of a young family sitting on the front porch of one the large homes. He read the faded scroll on the back. "*Rachel, Ned, Josie, little Ned, baby Ada-1920 in Southside, Birmingham*" The same young blonde woman was in the photograph, and his time her hair was shorter, and fell loosely about her shoulders. Rachel Montgomery wore her hair in the same loose style. The two women were identical. With hesitation, he came to the realization this young woman was Rachel, and she would never be found. Rachel Montgomery had died years before. Now, he had the task of ending the investigation of the disappearance of Rachel Montgomery.

Tom Meeks pick up the phone. "Mr. Neeley, there's no need to search for Rachel Montgomery any longer. She finally found her way home."

ABOUT THE AUTHOR

Judith M. McManus is a writer of historical southern fiction set primarily in the 19th and 20th centuries. She is the author of the bestselling novel, *The Music of Her Life* and her latest, *The Image of Rachel Clair*. Originally from Birmingham, Alabama, she now makes her home in the Atlanta area. To find out more about Judith and upcoming novels and events, follow her at judithmmcmanus.org or @JudithMMcManusAuthor (FB).

www.ingramcontent.com/pod-product-compliance
Lightning Source LLC
Chambersburg PA
CBHW020929310726
48980CB00007B/690/J